OPUS
MAGNUM

OPUS MAGNUM

VOLUME I

ABU KASEM

MAGNITUDE PUBLISHING

First published by Magnitude Publishing, 2019

Opus Magnum, Volume I

Abu Kasem asserts the right to be identified as the Author of the Work in accordance with the Copyright, Designs and Patents Act 1988.

A CIP catalogue record for this title is available from the British Library.

Visit the author's website at: www.abukasem.com

ISBN 978-1-911387-02-2

Foreskin

This book has not an introduction but a foreword; or an introduction of the foreword: yet not in any private space of yours, but into your mind and soul.

The Egyptians were looking for a hygienic measure that would eventually help them to palliate the effects of bilharzia; they chose the removal of the foreskin, a procedure known as circumcision.

It did not work at all; yet millions of little boys are still being exposed to wanton cuts.

This is the main reason why we decided to include a foreskin (foreword) for this marvellous and ever-expanding work of art.

Preface

Abu Kasem the Greedy Perfumer, and his vindictive observations on everything else.

An incredible account of what could have been, what could be, and what will be thought in a probable past, in an ignored present, and in an unlikely future by not so ordinary people who may have, that do and certainly shall exist in the endless possibilities of time... and space: the final frontier.

Some of the ideas written and developed here have been modified only to the extent to which we have been allowed. They have a life and an intention of their own, and there is nothing we can do to improve them if they were to refuse further expansion or manipulation.

Francis Bacon's *Essays*, LVIII. 'Salomon saith, There is no new thing upon the earth. So that as Plato had an imagination, that all knowledge was but remembrance; so Salomon giveth his sentence, that all novelty is but oblivion.'

Introduction

The *Opus Magnum* is an eternal account of all the history of things that were, are, and will be; those things that could have been, could be, and might occur in a probable future.

It is the sum of all thoughts, ideas, dreams, deliriums, aspirations, inspirations, and all you can think of that might spring out of the human brain and heart, that might be expressed in any written form in all the extension of time and the conceivable universes.

It is the most ambitious enterprise devised by any human who has ever existed, or does exist, or will-could-might exist in any probable future; its aim is sole but perhaps atrocious: to embrace within its pages all the events and thoughts and imaginations that occurred or could have occurred, that are taking place or could be, and those that shall happen and those that might never come into existence as well.

Conjure one thought in your mind, and you shall find it somewhere, within the eternal extension of this ever-expanding *Opus Magnum*.

Disclaimer

All mistakes regarding grammar have been consciously made.

All probable accuracies have been unconsciously realised.

The error is the prerogative of humans.

Only to the supra-human belongs the privilege of being right despite the apparent mistake.

Man and Life

I'm not a man... yet. I'm trying to become one, and also trying to become One. I see this as the only worthy task.

The rest is... nothing.

(Silence)

Man, me, I... all are singular terms that vainly attempt to define a complexity beyond imagination; but although a man is called a man (or a human, being), it does not imply he has yet become one (nor that the human is *being*)... or in One.

Who am I? Where am I going? What am I doing? (Besides writing and correcting these lines, of course.)

If mankind has a purpose, that purpose should be constant and conscious evolution. Yet this cannot be done in isolation.

Seek that which has to be found; that which exists in order to be found.

Similarities

I would be utterly delighted to share some remarkable observations made by John Peter Harrock XVI, who was not only famous owing to the noticeable lack of creativity found within his family regarding the name-choosing for those ill-fated circumstantial descendants, but who also was recognised as a great proto-sexologist and philatelist.

JPH XVI was born *circa* 1889 in his home near Sedona, in the state of Arizona, thanks to his parents, who had presumably copulated approximately nine months before the date of his birth; yet, this figure is contested by those who see in our hero's obsession with sex – which showed its first symptoms during his fourth year on this planet – an *obvious* and easy-to-infer eight-month pregnancy. Naturally, of course, we should also extend our gratefulness to both his sets of grandparents (which amounts to four), for being the procreators of John Peter Harrock's XVI mother and father; and to be fair, also to the meat-gods (parents) of his grandparents on both sides... (we decided to edit this enumeration because the family can be traced back to the times of Ramesses II).

His mother was obviously called Ophelia Lawson MCX, and his father was, predictably, John Peter Harrock XV.

We can plausibly infer, seeing both ancestors' names, that there was something else bonding them together besides the love of dark cigarettes and balloon fetish activities; though we are not quite sure what *that* was. If you do happen to know what *that* is, please write to 27 Meadowbridge Road THYRU4 GNJBI45938, Surrey, United Kingdom.

At the age of sixty-eight, JPH XVI finally understood, as if he had been touched by epiphanic muses, the inner alchemical relationship between the archaic and obsolete old school far-west duel and the vast universe of copulatory activities; or shall we say, **all** the physical and manual activities of a sexual nature, which he simply called physical manifestations of love.

Given the fact that the word *duel* is mentioned, we have to assume it embraces only the realm of men (as in male, binary, with a virile member made of flesh and a vast predominance of testosterone); be that of a hateful violent nature, or a sexual one.[1]

He believed that through this inspired agglomeration of ideas and intuitions that came down from the far beyond, he had, once and for all, found the missing link in the history of human sexuality; the trace that completed the circle of life and death, the scales that weighed love and hate; and the metal through which the coin of bliss and

---

1   It shall be up to the reader whether he or she will apply his remarkable findings to both genders, after reading the whole text.

anguish had been crafted. Thus he asserts it in his *Memoirs of a Forgetful Chap*:

> ... I was pondering about the striking similarity between those manifestations of love through our physicality, and the old-fashioned – and oftentimes effective – far-west revolver duellistic confrontation.[2]

In both cases, whether it is the scene fuelled by hatred or that one sweetened by love or salted by lust, we find a gun-revolver; albeit the materials from which the gun-weapon (due to sheer pragmatism we shall unify both of them under the name *revolver*) is made of might somehow – and ideally should – differ, they both possess the same essential qualities: they fire heated bullets, and they both can kill, and/ or bestow the gift of life.

In far east China, we can find the same analogy within the Taoist world, yet with a slight variation; whereas for us it's a revolver, for them it was (and is) a jade sword. It is yet to be demonstrated if those ill-fated yellow ones can fire bullets from a sword; their populace would indicate the bullet firing occurs from within a different source.

---

2   He clearly undermines the possibilities of orgiastic duels. "Love is a game wherein false creation and death penetrate each other, a game meant to be for only One... or for two at the most", he once stated in his diary.

The simple mathematical scope of logical intuition and chances shows us that in the aforementioned dual duellistic circumstance we can find one (or two, or three, or... continues *ad libitum et ad arbitrium*) of the following possibilities taking place, given the appropriate conditions for a confrontation fuelled by hatred or sweetened by love or salted through lust:

- Two proper revolvers, steel made or flesh made, well oiled, lubricated, and primarily clean.
- A proper steel revolver and a flesh-made one.
- A proper steel revolver and a plastic toy one.
- Two plastic-toy revolvers.
- One plastic-toy revolver, and a fleshy one.
- No revolvers at all, be they plastic toys, or steel ones or fleshy ones.
- A single duel (which would imply suicide or the simple shooting of bullets into the air) or a physical manifestation of self-love; it should be assumed that the presence of at least one revolver is a *conditio sine qua non*, be it metal or flesh made. If the circumstance requires it so, two hands shall be made of use... but preferably one's *own* hand/s.[3]

3　Some bits of information are missing, and we still cannot locate them, despite using *four* hands in the quest; though at *prima facie* that assertion sounds a bit too pretentious.

(It is worth mentioning the remarkable bravery and lack of prejudice that our champion shows, although having been raised in an oppressive and severe Catholic ambience, in not judging in *any* way whatsoever the physical love expressed between members of the same gender, nor by condemning the fruitful, exemplary and ever-teaching act of masturbation.)[4]

Notwithstanding the condition of the revolver or revolvers involved in the sacred ritual of destruction and creation, all sizes and measures can be found; hereby we shall find a few of those examples:

- Big (Monster, Enormous, Absolutely and Astonishingly Huge, Get the Fuck Out You Freak!, Third Leg, Short Barrel, Long Barrel, Thickness depending on the calibre, *ad libitum ad abundantiam*)
- Small (Almost Normal, Tiny, Ungrabbable, Are You Serious?, Hilarious, Ethereal, Short Barrel, Thinness depending on the calibre, *ad libitum ad fundum*)

---

4   Thanks to this editorial observation we can assume with a high degree of certainty that the scope of his findings embraces all genders, as per doubt expressed in footnote 1.

Intriguingly, or not really given that Mother Nature knows better,[5] they all possess a unique and bonding quality:

They can all *kill.*

The one and only necessary condition is to possess a good pulse and the almost divine skill to know:

- When, Where, and Whom to shoot and wound or kill.[6]
- Whether one (or several) bullet(s) is/are worth being spent. Death can sometimes be achieved through a bullet-less – or dry – encounter. Be that alone, under a Self-Love regime, or in Duel-mode.[7]

Therefore, I can infer that the virtuosity lies within the skill of the gun holder in question, leaving the matter of size, shape, calibre and shininess to be discussed by shallow and slow-witted people who know nothing about the true nature of love and death.

A single name should suffice as an eternal proof of this: that of Mud Spencer, who once

---

5   Those probably are his first documented signs of bipolarity.

6   Abu Ibn Simwahhab, Saracen erudite, scholastic and mystic expert firmly thinks that such a formula links our protagonist with an unknown Texan Sufi order. The original formula is: Place, Time and People.

7   Again, the ever-present Taoist influence becomes notable.

was a famous and handsome sheriff during those innocent years throughout my own childhood (a sort of James Bond of the time), whose name frequently inhabited the dry mouths of the local Westerners due to the fact that he had a really super tiny and laughable revolver; never did his many mistresses nor did the more than a thousand vile men stuffed by his silver-pointed bullets ever complain about such a tiny detail; love and death always find their ways, albeit usually ignored by men.

Giving thorough detail to the mathematical scope of possibilities that may occur when a duellistic confrontation takes place, and remembering that not all deaths are accountable on bullets – be those silver-headed, platinum-headed, diamond-headed, king diamond, *ad libitum ad honorem*, or sticky-milky ones – I've managed to unearth and enumerate the following feasible combinations:

- One dies at: the hand, both hands, the tongue, the lips, the bullet/s or bullet-less revolver, or at the foot, the feet, the elbow, *ad libitum ad mortem* of the other.
- The duel is deathless.

- Both die (this is hard to achieve because of the precision and practice involved and the patience required).[8]

Also, we shall enumerate the types of shooters by the speed at which the bullet or bullets are expelled:

- Early shooter: In this case, the triggering occurs whilst the revolver is still inside the holster or pants.
- Fast shooter: The bullet/s are expelled with no time to aim properly, sometimes landing thus staining the leg or worn garments; Shakespeare might have been one of the most celebrated artists suffering from this condition.
- Average shooter: The spit of his bullet/s might arrive a second earlier or later, but he complies with regular standards.
- Delayed shooter: Probably due to health issues or not, his bullet/s arrive way too late in order to make the proper kill.

---

8   The famous film critic from the Pampas, Agustín González, implies that John McClane, the forgettable character from the blockbuster film *Die Hard,* could have had a chronic syndrome known as the retarded or lazy bullet. For those slow witted, he just could not ejaculate. Which probably implies he also was always late to his meetings or rendezvouses. Yet, the question imposes itself: what if the whole purpose of the supposedly Christmas movie is to make us aim for a death that occurs whilst being literally hard, erect?

- Shooter *in absentia*: Due to lack of bullet/s, or so called lazy sticky milky chaps, the outcome never... occurs.[9]

It is noted that anxiety plays a huge role in each one of the above-mentioned cases.
On the other extreme, we find the:

- Shooter *in absentia*: Due to a lack of bullet/s, or to the so-called sticky milky lazy bastards, the outcome never takes place. Also referred to as the *dry-mate*. This being the case, his or her[10] lover might die of boredom. This way of dying is sometimes preferable.[11]

Dear reader, if this *cumulus nimbus* of words makes no sense to you, please, worry not. Nobody ever accepted his extroverted theories; but, for the sake of curiosity, let's carry on unfolding his wretched mindless inquiries:

...the curious detail is that the formal ejaculation is, for the metaphoric French speakers-writers, *la petite mort*, or the "little death" if you prefer. I ignore whether they see themselves as everlasting

---

9   Yes, the use of the word come would have created a very predictable pun of sorts.

10 10 Squirting, or in its absence the mere dewiness, should be regarded as the female bullet.

11 If on the footnote (1) he began to show signs of bipolarity, this is a probable sign of dementia.

poets, or whether they actually consider the sticky milky substance to be composed of very tiny little men and women trying not to drown in the intensity of the feminine ocean... Shakespeare used to caress the page with his immortal pen (or did he use a feather pen? Or did he perhaps make use of a knife as a writing device? Yet, alas, if the latter were the preferred choice for the reader who is now immersed in a sort of *choose your own writing device*, the verb *caress* should be immediately discarded due to the proper lack of information regarding the Bard's dexterity with sharpened objects), casting words or neologisms upon his creator's canvas, inventions such as:

Helena replies, being in love with Demetrius: "... To die upon the hand I love so well." *A Midsummer Night's Dream*, Act II

This famous line clearly suggests that Helena was a transvestite, or a sort of freak of nature, or a not-so-common hermaphrodite. I hope at least she might have cleaned it up (the hand) before the play was over. Bipolarity should not be discarded; nor should the suggestion that the expression *petite mort* can be suitable to describe the feminine experience, as it is claimed by some that women can achieve such climaxes of pleasure.

"Cowards die many times before their deaths; the valiant never taste[12] of death but once." *Julius Caesar*, Act II

I am glad to be a coward, and so is my wife. In fact, I wouldn't recommend the exercise of such a valorous virtue, because the risk of death (of the lover implied) by asphyxia, inner drowning or by whichever means you, dearest reader, shall be able to conjure in your own mind, might occur after that forgotten gesture of expulsion: the density and copious amount of that which shall be expelled from a revolver (whether it is a meaty, metallic, or *ad libitum ad aeternum* one) that has never tasted the fervour and heat of a seminal bullety downpour (or up-pour or side-pour, depending on the final position) in a lifetime of not-dying. Terrifying. A sticky milky death indeed.

"To be or not to be... To die: to sleep." *Hamlet*, Act 3, famous monologue

Irrefutable scientific facts embedded in a wonderful play. We all know about the slumber-like mood that tends to occur after the masculine

---

12 It is commented that the author claimed: "Whoever tastes the seed of his own death more than once, is surely a man with devious tendencies." He also asserted that all true masculinity implied the tasting of that which all men desire to experience through the lover's mouth.

petite mort. Following the modernisation frenzy in which we are submerged, a newly adapted version of *Hamlet* has been forwarded to a renowned West End theatre in London. The slight variation in the world-famous monologue reads thus:

"To die: I shall call you a taxi, so then I can proceed to wolf down a pepperoni pizza and finally to sleep like a motherfucker."[13]

Hamlet, feeling the burning effects of poison.

"O, I die, Horatio."

We can perfectly infer that either Horatio was a voyeur, or that Hamlet was an exhibitionist, or both;[14] or perhaps that the Dane was fond of Horatio in some fashion that went beyond a regular standard friendly and platonic relationship that should be expected among members of the masculine realm, thus sharing the product of his dairy burst.

---

13 The matinee version of the new revision replaced this offensive term with *champ*, which is a much more acceptable one.

14 Since Hamlet utters his friend's name, it is perfectly clear that he was aware of his presence; therefore, we can state that Hamlet *was* indeed an exhibitionist who, if he were to be alive today, surely would be making a livelihood through webcam shows and Snapchat live broadcasts.

"I should not die but in Jerusalem." *Henry IV*, Part 2

What a freak. Disgusting, abominable, repulsive and blasphemous behaviour; such a man should be dispossessed of his place in history. To imagine the international conflict that such a statement could engender in the current world, inundates me with dread and terror.

"Killing myself, to die upon a kiss." *Othello*, final scene

We are all aware of the beast that rose (or perhaps it was always there, alive, dormant, expectant) within Othello, instigated by the catalyst evil of Iago; but under my interpretation of death, he becomes a pervert, an animal, a wretched beast. How could he ever perform such a reprehensible act on a death maiden; Desdemona's gelid lips against a heated stickiness that came from his Moorish curved revolver, as a reprehensible consequence of the act of self-love inspired by the mere thought of a kiss.[15] We have to bestow upon the ill-fated

---

15 Leonhard Ciccioli, reputed Italo-Austrian psychiatrist, points out that the inspiring stimulus could be a proof of Othello's emotional immaturity. In his deep words: "No seasoned lover would ever climax at the thought of a mere kiss."

twofold traitor (for he also abandoned his faith and origin) some credit for being able to fire even though his lover was already dead; a tendency toward necrophilia shan't be disregarded.

The list could go on *ad nauseam*, but I simply don't feel like quoting too much; and since my digestive system is working very well, such a path is quite foreign to me.

I will finish my brilliant exposition with William Shakespeare's love lines that find their abode in his eternal *Much Ado About Nothing*'s final part, when Benedick (the perfect mix of Italian and English wording here makes quite a combo)[16] replies lovingly to Beatrice:

"I will live in thy heart, die in thy lap, and be buried in your eyes…"

I only hope, dearest Benedick, that you have at least washed Beatrice's dress – or her legs – depending on the scope and reach of the burst. As I also hope and pray that it was not his intention to watch his beloved rub the sticky milky substance *inside* her eyes; whereas most men want to aim or see their bullets on – or inside – their lover's mouth, apparently this chap had quite an eccentric preference.

---

16 For those ignorant bastards who require an explanation, such a combo literally means goodcock, or goodpenis, or gooddick *ad libitum ad coitus interruptus.*

But, dear friends, let's return now to our first duel anal...ogy.

Sorry, got a bit confused.

Perchance the best option is for both lovers to see the light at the same time; to die together; to reach the highest peaks of Eros and Venus bonded in an inner flood that surrenders the Egos, thus dissolving the separateness into the realm of the Truth, like two raindrops becoming one with the ever-present and embracing ocean. But it takes time, practice and patience. And time. And patience with patience.

Patience is of the essence, and obviously, several duellistic confrontations are needed to perfect the aiming skills and other secrets of the Arts of Love.

Impatience is the force that shuts down not only the few chances one might have to learn, but also the wind that might close the legs of your lover, and the wind that dries her inner waters; also, it can be the chilly current that tenderises your revolver.

As Ali, the Lion of Islam used to say, there are three things that cannot be recovered:

- The arrow that has parted from the bow
- The word uttered unthinkingly
- The missed opportunity

In the same manner, beloved learner-reader, I can tell you that bullets are not eternal, nor infinite; they can, and surely will, be somehow wasted. Take good care of them, but nevertheless, take heed: exercise your will to such an extent that you become the master of time, the master of the trigger. Practise dry; that is, practise by keeping the essence inside, both when you are alone and with your beloved. Practise until you become one with the practice itself – and perhaps you might finally become nothingness; then, you will be totally *in absentia* for the world but absolutely present for yourself and Love, inhabiting a realm where bullets, revolvers, dry, sticky-milky substances, are going to be nothing but sounds, echoes of a past experience (dreamlike) when death and life were separated.[17]

Draw it out fast, and *then* consider whether the bullet is worth being fired; aim for consciousness in the shooting: remember that the goal is that gun, bullet and aim become one... until you realise that there is no revolver or ammunition or "separation".

---

17 In the same manner, the film critic Agustín González noted the apologetic antagonism between this wise piece of advice and the Hollywood propaganda that surreptitiously installs in our minds the concept (alas, illusion) that bullets are everlasting and infinite. Suffice to watch dreadful examples such as *Rambo, Commando, ad libitum ad plumbum.*

Sometimes the circumstance is not worth the shot. To recognise when, where and with whom to do it, depends on you.

John Peter Harrock XVI died in his sleep, accompanied by the persistent company of a little burning candle and the dim light it offered; his ninety-seven years of age caressing his soul; his bullet-less wrinkled revolver inside his suede holster; his departure mirrored his entrance into this world: empty, and with no Ego left to be expelled.

Editor's Note:
It is worth noting the striking similarity within three concepts that, at random, could be thought of as having nothing in common: love, evolve and revolver. Also worthy of our attention is the depth of the author's insight, and the lack of improvisation in the choosing of such a word to describe a cornerstone of the masculine society: the revolver as the ultimate weapon of love, death and life. The giver of evolving chances, and the ultimate manifestation of union among humans.

God

FROM A POPULAR FOLK TALE:

A man went to Nasrudin and demanded: "Nasrudin, you are a clever man and you are an esoteric. If you're really as clever as you think you are, then show me God."

Nasrudin, who was tending to his garden, casually picked up a stone and threw it, hitting the man square on the head. The man ran away, moaning in pain. He went straight to the village judge and complained to him about what just occurred.

The judge called in Nasrudin, and reprimanded him: "Nasrudin, you are a learned man. That was an awful thing to do. He asked you a perfectly reasonable question. Why couldn't you give him a reasonable answer?"

"What is his complaint?" asked Nasrudin.

"He came to me and complained that you hit him on the head with a rock. Now he is in terrible pain," replied the judge.

Nasrudin was quick to respond: "Excellent. Now if this man will just show me the pain, then I will show him God."

Final Debate

"Jesus was human, but with divine bonds," some asserted.

"Jesús was my neighbour, a nice little chap," said Vicente del Cilantro, the fruit-seller of a little village located two miles south of Foz, in Lugo.

"Jesus was God trapped within flesh," thus asserted the Roman Catholic Apostolic Church.

"Jesus was (is) a Master inspired by Divinity," so the Sufis assert.

"Jesus is the Messiah," foresaw Melchior +2.

But prominent professors of the Oxford College for Religious Research and Erudite Speculatory Intuitions assert with no hint of a doubt that Jesus was an ant. In order to prove it, they quote the Gospel of Thomas: "…lift up the stone, and you will find me there."

Other scholars insist on lingering in the insect realm, quoting the same Gospel: "…split a piece of wood; I am there."

As a natural consequence of such a belief, they consider that He was a termite.

Another adventurous assertion pronounced – and it is still resounding in the most prestigious cloisters throughout the world – not without a hint of adolescent rebelliousness, that: "Jesus was a rat."

In order to prove this point, that tiny but very influential think-tank/religious-extravaganza called the Mickey Mouse Religious Club, quotes Tahir Shah's wondrous opus, *Sorcerer's Apprentice*, page 280:

> "...Just like that temple – Karnidevi, near Bilkaner – where they worship rats. I've heard there are thousands of the little fellows. Devotees flock to the temple from across India. They feed the rats great trays of food. Only when the rodents can devour no more, do the pilgrims eat what they've left."

For the Mickey Mouse Religious Club, a despicable rodent-obsessed sect, the above-mentioned extract serves as irrefutable proof for their religious *motto*; this pseudo-scholastic organisation firmly believes that Jesus went to die (predictably) in India. They are fervent readers, though at this point we should better say reciters, of two particular books: *Christ in Kashmir* by Aziz Kashmiri and *Jesus Lived in India* by Holger Kersten; works that support their unique vision of the Nazarene visiting this part of Gondwana's soil.

According to them, the rodent-infested temple in India is a symbol of the multiplied and eternised

Master, not in bread and fish, but in rats.[18] The trays of food serve as a symbolic last supper, and we, humans, are only worthy of the remains, as perpetual sinners.

Their basic theology also includes a disgusting set of practices such as reprehensible orgies: horrid rites performed by all the male parishioners – which is to say the *entirety* of the congregation because they deem women to be lesser beings – where men disguised as cats are sodomised by members of the sect who predictably dress up and act like rodents. After the unwelcome posterior visit comes to an end (or dies, if you fancy Shakespeare) all the parishioners feast on cheese, until the first morning bird announces the waking sun.

As a consequence of simple logical formulae, the cat is seen as the cause of all Evil; any feline representation is but a countenance of the multifaceted devilish figure that dwells in the bottom of Hell, which in this case consists not of fire, but of boiling oceanic waters swarming with an eternal overpopulation of tuna fish.

Any cartoon with a cat in a lead role is of course forbidden, as well as other references to felines throughout the history of art; all products and creations that are not to be enjoyed

---

18 Some apocryphal versions suggest that Walter Disney was the founder and benefactor of this extravagant sect. If we made room to allow such shocking information, his cartoonish creation would project a different shadow over the entertainment industry; not only did he give voice to the first version of the animated rodent, but this character eventually became his number one hit, in addition to playing a vital role in the development of his own frozen empire of today.

by the parishioners under any circumstance whatsoever.[19] The most conservative wing of the movement is planning a massive boycott of *Cats* and any play related in any way or fashion to Andrew Lloyd Webber, who is thought by many, not only those belonging to the conservative faction, to be himself a cat.

Just as it is always the case with any group of people that congregate around a shared idea or belief – whether or not there are costumes involved in the etiquette – several factions start to appear, thus fragmenting the formerly known harmonic union; a small sect within this horrid group of fanatics believe, inspired by his unending appetite for cats, that the hairy little chap from Melmac, better known as Alf, is the final Messiah, the secret Knight of the Apocalypse that shall arrive to install the Kingdom of the Lord all over this planet of sinners.[2021]

The last step that leads us beyond this realm of mind-puzzling cheese mayhem of orgiastic cartoon-like extravagant theories is taken – shyly albeit with certain

---

19 Among these we can find: Garfield, Tom, Puss in Boots, He-Man's Gringer; apparently, the hard wing of the sect is starting to ban all human actors that have given their voices to cat characters, such as Antonio Banderas. It is also important to remark that before his Islamic conversion, Yusuf Islam was also forbidden.

20 If you would like to know more about this rodental sect which might benefit from, in a near future, the very protection of the Vatican, do not under any circumstance stop reading this collection of incredible writings, properly known as *Opus Magnum*, because a complete detailed description of this *à la mode* worship is due to be written...

21 An excellent reason not to print this dossier, and to only publish it in e-format. Thus, the rats will never be able to destroy the unspoken truths by eating them.

comforting security – by a very small[22] sect within the Oxford College for Religious Research and Erudite Speculatory Intuitions, which call themselves the…[23]

Their members (it is not quite clear whether this refers to the actual persons from which the *members* were taken, or to some sort of *speaking body parts*) state that those lines previously quoted from the Gospel of Thomas are actually a type of secret metaphorical code[24] that naturally leads us to the conclusion that Jesus, in reality, is Pinocchio, and God our Father is Geppetto.

Of course, if this were true, then why was Jesus crucified, if he himself was made of the same material as the cross?

Wouldn't that be a despicable redundancy?

PS: a vast array of conspiracy theories obsessively surround the Mickey Mouse Religious Club; we choose at random one that suggests such sect might be lobbying in favour of using cats in lab tests rather than mice.

---

22 According to secret diaries found in an obscure and sinful pub in Canterbury, it is formed by only three members: a right arm, a left leg and a nose.

23 Something may have been lost in translation (Ed.).

24 Referring to the piece of wood and to Jesus, both in Gospel of Thomas.

Consufion

> "Shakespeare's name is sometimes rendered in perfectly correct and acceptable Persian as *Sheikh-Peer*, 'the ancient sage'."
> *The Sufis*, Idries Shah. Page 267.

D espite the numerous biographies of the great English writer that could have been, can, and shall be written – and those which could have been, are being, and will be retrieved – the real cause of the Bard's death was, is, and will continue to be an inextricable mystery.

Lord van Bronckhorst, a reputed gardener from Sutton who has never in his life heard nor read a single word about Shakespeare, firmly believes that his death was due to a virulent fever that he might have caught during a recreational night; perchance, according to the venturous theory of the Lord, it was all due to his refusal to wear a coat (when in fact the weather demanded it) in order to show to the *femmes* present at the time that his blood still flowed like that of a muscular and spirited chap. The gardener then proceeded to prepare for us a delicious *boeuf bourguignon*, for which he also offered us the recipe. But, since it is clearly off topic, we refused to replicate it here: yet, the meal was lovely.

Sir Arthur Stephanek (also known by his students as *spaghetti*), professor of English Literature and Semiotics at the University of Bologna, not only agrees on the feverish cause, but on something else that, for being so obvious and simple, could have passed unnoticed by the common mortal:

> "....he surely must have died due to something very, very grave..."

But for Sir Arthur and Lord van Bronckhorst, not all paths are full of scented roses, given that the distinguished and celebrated Knight of the Order of Templar Alta Orbis, emeritus Knight of the Council of the Guardians of the Oral and Written Tradition of the Heirs to the Chest belonging to the deeply Transformed Lord of the Multiple Rings and Secretary of the United Kingdom's foreign affairs, Sir Richard Hamilton Roberts Angus Podgorny of the Hills Saint Martin Cafrune von Holstein Bettersburs Perez Carrillo of Scotland von Ulm, thinks otherwise.

He, Sir Richard Hamilton Roberts Angus Podgorny of the Hills Saint Martin Cafrune von Holstein Bettersburs Perez Carrillo of Scotland von Ulm, turned out to be a stubborn opponent regarding the real reason for the ancient sage's death.

In his *Memoirs*, a rather disturbed Sir Richard Hamilton Roberts Angus Podgorny of the Hills Saint Martin Cafrune von Holstein Bettersburs Perez Carrillo of Scotland von Ulm conveys his thoughts on the matter:

I can firmly affirm, despite being constantly upset and shaken by this bloody Honshu Island and its unpredictable earthquakes, that Lord William Shakespeare died from a terrible and violent strike on his cheek, it having been inflicted by his lover's mother.

The origin or cause?

The stain of semen that shamefully ruined her daughter's dress; I have indeed discussed this with my departed friend John Peter Harrock XVI; and when he had finished tasting my idea, he immediately spat at my face a line that reinforced not only his ejaculatory speculations, but mine as well:

"I will live in thy heart, die in thy lap, and be buried in your eyes..."

Here the possible significances multiply *ad infinitum, ad libitum, ad imaginatus, ad coitus non interruptus.*

Accepting our death-ejaculation theory, we can assert with no hesitation that this expelling episode – the spat of the one-eyed boneless Chinese – must have been a premature one, given the landing place of the sticky milky substance;[25] though I have to admit, thus making room for my scientific self, that the voluntary aiming at the dress shan't be discarded lightly.

If that had been the case, one would be entitled to ask: Why? Why? Why? Why? Was Shakespeare fond of fabric? Perhaps her dress had a naughty stamp on it, thus provoking his big-bang? Is she to blame?

Could it be that the lady in question had a dress fetish, and having attached herself that much to a simple piece of material asked him to die on her lap? If he did not shoot, then who did? Were they alone? Was there a voyeur enjoying the scene? Could the voyeur – surely enjoying some manual carnal pleasure himself – have ignited this incident through a ricochet-style climax, thus becoming the *real* Keith Hernandez?

Interrupting for a brief moment the gracious flow of his *Memoirs* for the sake of a brief interjection, in the next paragraph we appreciate how committed he was to the scientific method and ruthless logical scrutiny when Sir Richard Hamilton Roberts Angus Podgorny of the Hills Saint Martin Cafrune von Holstein Bettersburs Perez Carrillo of Scotland von Ulm leaves no stone unturned... therefore bound to find Jesus, the saviour of humanity:

---

25 Should be read as an *homage* to John Peter Harrock.

What if the stain was not produced by that manly substance, but by a similar-looking liquid – albeit not similar in taste – such as mayonnaise? How should I know the difference between the taste of that sticky milky substance and the French egg-based invention? Given the shyness of our literary hero, all of the above – including the mere possibility that the stain had been never produced in the first place by Shakespeare himself nor by any type of sticky substance, milky or of another nature – cannot and shall not be ruled out.

And if perhaps his shyness was indeed a façade whose only purpose was to conceal his naughty and reprehensible aiming-at-dress habits (a fetish of sorts, shall we say?), and he actually did die on her lap thus ruining her garment – and reputation – *ad aeternum*?

That's it; he was an anxious little chap, inexperienced and eager to let his dense substance greet the world and bid farewell to his own round – and swollen, we assume – and hairy vessel, thus showing a complete disregard for others people's efforts and work, represented here by her soon-to-be-thrown-out-to-the-pigs pink dress. How do I know that the dress was pink? Who am I to say that the pink was dress? And what if the dress was yellow? Or orange?

What if the wearer of the infamous dress was not a girl but merely a man, in this particular event he being Shakespeare, in solitude, resorting to his feminine side; perhaps wearing the dress to be stained, perchance making use of such a garment as a sensitive depiction of his yin side, and he was just playing the old *five-against-one* game (thank you, Mr G.), fulfilling the aim of all love which is unity, marrying himself through his hand – or hands depending on the self-loving technique used – thus sealing such alchemical ceremony with a splash on his *own* lap covered by the pink garment?

Was, is and will this be an affair that couldn't, isn't and will not be solved?

For these and many other reasons (according to my calculations, those *other* reasons reached the sum of 1.786.984 and then died due to a most certain lack of oxygen) it is our duty to embark ourselves to navigate upon the infinite waters of plausible interpretations; these become richer in meaning with every gasp of air.

We[26] can also affirm without fear (but why not with a bit of fright? Isn't it normal for a man

---

26 So far, we have not mentioned prior usage of the plural form because we intended to use the "We" as the main example. It is still debated whether the use of the plural is due to his habit of writing whilst being surrounded by enormous numbers of people, or because he simply was the visible face of a sage's sect; or rather all of this was due to his metaphysical and esoteric knowledge about the multiple personalities that inhabit a single body and use a single name to encompass and depict the fragmented nature of the human being.

to be afraid, to cry, to eat its own mucus and then drink its own urine?) of *erratum*, that Will Shake[27] predicted his very own death. If this were, is and shall be the case, I would rather put on the suit and hurry up because I am about to miss the 9 o'clock train and I can't afford to be late again given that I am about to lose my job; but if this had been, is, and will be the *case* – a certain number of actions sustained in time that produce a certain effect – time travel shan't be ruled out, because as far as we know, a person, regardless of its genius, is not yet able to produce verses after being mortally slapped in the face by his supposed or actual or soon-to-be mother-in-law.

For the sake of science and all those things of which the relentless logic is deserving, this question should and has to be formulated:

What if WS was a zombie? Or a Highlander who could only die if his head were chopped

---

27 Rock and Art critic Ludovico Manpiero suggests that if William Shakespeare were alive today and had chosen the guitar instead of the feather pen, his band should have been named Will and the Pear Shakes.

off?[28] Following this lead, a supposed-to-be-mortal slap on the cheek could have not sufficed. Did his mother-in-law know about his zombie/ Highlander status, and slapped him *à dessein* for the sake of Divine knowledge and the benefit of all humanity? I'm afraid: yes, this is what I feel and I announce it because I am a mucus-eating man who is not frightened of being afraid and to thus state that perchance she is the true heroine of our tale.

Or maybe, just *maybe*, I am dead as well and this is simply my reflection – or the echo of my own self – pondering about memories long ago forgotten whilst being trapped in the never-ending karmic cosmic loop; but if the memories

---

28 It is interesting to note that the German historian Manfred Hubert Eichert thinks that the origin of eunuchs could have something to do with the belief in Highlanders as immortal beings. He proposes: "Eunuchs are probably the victims of a half-belief in those amazing immortal creatures, mythical ones, symbolic of the renewed and wise man who dies before death comes to get him. Probably through the arts of fate or chance, these ill-fated nutless bastards were surely confused for those mythical creatures, the Highlanders, and as a consequence suffered the amputation of their head (southern one); though unfortunately for them, sometimes the knife would travel further south to encompass the whole package." Others, like the expert in paganism and brutality Jaime Sittar, think that "...they were castrated because they could not completely believe in the myth of the Highlander, hence they recurred to a mathematical solution: If half of the myth is accepted, then, we should cut the middle head, that is, that which is located in the equator of the man's body." It is worth noting that both experts ignored the basic fact that, in general, eunuchs were only deprived of their testicles, and nothing more.

are susceptible of being forgotten, how can I be reading them, and writing them, and sharing them with my beloved readers? Are they, I mean *you*, deceased as well? Is it a nightmare? Is it a dream?

Are they (not you) really memories, and I've simply convinced myself of something which has not happened, tricked myself into believing in things that I have not yet experienced, and populated my life with those experiences like a greedy piggy banker? Do memories have an owner, or is it just a capitalist's illusion to own the memory of the universe, the wisdom and recollections of all those who have trod, are treading, and will tread on this earth?

Have I taken too many pills? Nurse? Mother? Banana?

Maybe he dreamed of that dying-slapping episode, wrote those immortal lines, and only then the tragedy unfolded: a premonitory dream. What if Shakespeare stole the dreams of others and thus wrote his immortal opus? Do we know as a fact that the bard was not suffering from insomnia?

Then, if night after night he failed to seduce Morpheus and repose in slumber, how the hell did he write his works? That's it: he never wrote a thing, and simply was used by some sages who made him pose as a writer, when in fact he was a lonely, anxious and pretentious chap. Again, for the sake of science and good manners, another awkward, earth-shaking, ground-breaking question shall be uttered:

What if Shakespeare, during his endless insomniac nights, thought that he had been the dreamer of a dream that never really caressed his brain but was only believed to have occurred? What if also William was as unstable as I am right now, and nothing of what we wrote, said and spat could be taken for granted? What if he was a eunuch and could never produce any sticky milky substance?

If that had been the case (I don't care, I missed the train and besides, I hated my job), did he use a mayonnaise tube to replace his own minuscule swimming friends whose abode is that binary roundness which serves as a perfect metaphor of our planet Earth? Could Pinocchio have something to do with the slapping-semen affair?

Am I right? Am I wrong? Left? Up? Down? In chains? Alice? But, if I were, am, or will be in chains, how come (give me a dress please) these lines are being written? Is it all in my mind?

I could be perfectly insane, and in need of another dose of my daily pills. Who knows? What I do know is that he, known by his innermost circle as William Stanislao Shakespeare, could have died some long moments *after* the slapping, thus enjoying a divine period of grace that gave him the required time to write the play in which that eternal line is included (read above if your memory fails, thank you). If this was what eventually happened, then it is more than likely that the executed Hladík may have dreamt himself being a certain taciturn South American writer, composing a short story entitled *The Secret Miracle*.

Or probably William never existed at all, and was a creation of a group of sages who needed him, a grey and taciturn ignorant peasant, to be their visible face, placed in and imbued with heavenly and transcendent wisdom, thus to serve a higher purpose rather than ejaculating on barely legal teenagers. An awkward sensation of *déjà vu* invades myself.

What if he never managed to feel any sort of attraction for females? Or he never died–spat that milky sticky substance, because he was a eunuch? (I've just realised I used that theory once; but was it *me* who thought about it? Was it here? Or was it simply a dream in which Hladík whispered to Borges that Christopher Nolan told me – allegedly – to write the word eunuch?)

What if that lass was not wearing a dress at all, and everything is a figment of my imagination? Or there was no mother-in-law, no little girlfriend, and he was just producing delirious thoughts during one of his night wanderings? What if I'm really insane? Have I written that already? Or is it just an illusion?

And what if I fucking stop asking *What if?*

Anyway, we do know at least that he has been, is, and will be properly, completely and irrefutably dead; which might be true, of course, provided the fact that he ever did exist; and, predictably, under the condition that we do really exist, and we read, and we write, and we eat our own mucus. If you are ready to accept that William Stanislao Shakespeare is either a zombie or a Highlander, I would suggest that you part in a quest for him, starting in the Hindu Kush.

All we can affirm, with a certainty of about 58.790%, is that his sticky milky prediction came true. In the same way that our great Jorge Luis Borges foresaw his own blindness, and Beethoven foreheard his own deafness, and Toscanini predicted his own name, and – surely – Mickey always knew deep inside that he was *not* meant to be Mortimer but much more than a simple metaphorical cartoon. He was, is, and will be, the true Messiah. Hail Mickey!

But again, I shall not allow myself to become deranged, and we shall walk back again on the path of good Will, brandishing the protective spear of love and truth.

Death duplicated itself, both as an irremovable stain on a young girl's dress (or was it a boy? But, if he was a boy, why was he wearing a dress? Perhaps he was so attached to his mother that he was impersonating her.

Yes! That could have been the case; sometimes, I myself like wearing a couple of old fashioned dresses to do some shopping at the town market. Is it wrong?!?!?) and scattered in The Ancient Sage's ashes (again, please, if you lost track, up you shall go and read once more).

But, were those Shakespeare's remains in the form of ashes, buried in her lover's eyes?[29] Was she really deadly deceased at the moment of the ashes' entrance? Or was she alive, and as a consequence was left blind, prefacing Borges' own fate? Was she somehow related to the great Argentine?

Just between us, some say that the girl's (or whatever shape she/he/it had) mother, at the exact time of the slap (probably it was 17:89 p.m. BST) was seventeen years of age. Then, how old was the supposed dress-bearer? Could all be explained by the Worm-Alice-Higgins Effect? If this were the case, then it's perfectly reasonable – and feasible – that the daughter was older than the mother her/him/it/self.

Shortly after this last page of his, Sir Richard Hamilton Roberts Angus Podgorny of The Hills Saint Martin Cafrune von Holstein Bettersburs Perez Carrillo of Scotland von Ulm died. It was, is and will be believed, that the cause of his parting had something to do with what

---

29 5 See *Similarities* in this same opus.

neurologists call *Cerebrum Chronon*. The organ ends up devouring itself through a series of paradigmatic thoughts and theories.

Others claim that the insomnia-ridden nights helped to aggravate his condition: wet, partly cloudy and densely sticky.

It is of the utmost importance to remember, in order to understand this whole theoretical mess, that during Shakespeare's time it was wildly and widely believed that semen stains were impossible to remove. They used to be referred to as the *sticky milky doom*. Thus, we are provided with a feasible motif that caused the supposed-to-be-deadly slap.

Origins

The famous theologian and member of the Royal College of Theological Studies, Sir Rigobert Angus Buss (who by the way was always full, especially during rush hours and after meals) feels in his heart of hearts – especially during his morning toothbrushing ritual – that he is quite deserving of a place in the pantheon of the champions of Theology; hence, he offers us a quite groundbreaking[30] and, why not, risky theory that would eventually prove to be the key to his scholar Olympus:

> If Pinocchio were Jesus, or Jesus were Pinocchio,[31] or the other way around, the mere idea of a crucifixion *per se* would be (and is) an awful and despicable redundancy; and given that God shan't be regarded

---

30 It is said that the man who read his complete theory for the first time fell into an abyss that opened just where he was sitting, or standing, or jumping, or crawling (Ed.).

31 This footnote has nothing to say about the matter. Yet, it would help your understanding of the current text enormously if you read the previous chapters.

as a second-class poet or artist, I feel obliged to propose and produce an alternative approach to religion's most famous crime, which I do sincerely believe took place in some other fashion; it is my contention that the lavish and inevitable crime-sacrifice could have been hand produced.

It is due to my profound connection with the Lord, that I am able to utter this sentence:

Instead of being predictably left to die on the cross, the wooden Messiah – having been spared the torment that the supposedly *faux* flesh-and-blood Jesus did suffer – was fiercely induced to perform the act of masturbation or self-love through frantic and lustful movements until, as a natural consequence of two wooden ends under friction, fire, one of the many faces of the unnameable dark enemy, made its scorching appearance, thus burning the Master to death, releasing us from the unbearable weight of the original sin.[32]

---

32 Certain elites within the Vatican are beginning to quote this theory in order to help the understanding of why such a selfish activity is condemned by the official Church. Also, a group of scientists under the protection of the holy state are trying to elucidate the weight of the Original Sin (soon to appear in these same pages – Ed.). But as always happens, confrontation arises in every social movement; in this case, opposing those who ban the selfish act of self-love, we find the mystic sect called *Pinocchieros,* fervent adepts of that lavish self-love manual activity. The cornerstone of the *corpus* of their belief is that salvation and enlightenment are due to come, paradoxically, through masturbatory explosion; the expelling of the masculine seed, if performed during a set of complex prayers, should produce the instant transcendence and resurrection, which in this particular case would transform the devoted man of flesh and bone into a wise wooden doll.

God proves, even without the necessity to do so, to be the father of all poets, the ancestor of all dramatists and play writers, creating everlasting life through death. I myself, an expert in Provençal and French, can assure you, dear readers, that the origin of the expression *la petite mort* finds its birth in this act of divine love: *la grande mort*. Life through death. How fucking poetic is that shit, man?

Once we accept these facts, the natural question arises:

What was it that helped the Master make that passionate self-sacrifice possible?[33] What helped him raise his weapon in order to conquer death? Is that the possible origin of the legend of Parsifal and the spear that guarded the Holy Grail? What was he thinking of? Is it a blasphemy to tread on those squally paths?

---

33 Notably, we can also infer the fabled tampering that occurred within the realm of storytelling; the infamous alteration of the growing limb in Pinocchio's nature. Originally, according to historian Lord Gerard Lukinson, "that which grew through the force of a lie, was not his nose but his penis". If this were to be true, the *lie* becomes the path towards Death and posterior salvation of the human race. This reinforces the Vatican's condemnation of the lustful and solitary act. "The lie is the path that leads to eternal doom. Thou shall not lie, but if Thou liest, Thou shan't answer nature's call. If Thou shall succumb to the temptation of the blood, the blazing fires of Hell shall be thine eternal doom.

If I'm the one on whom lies the obligation to answer, I would say that the love he felt for humanity inspired his bodily reaction, which ultimately made the self-amatorial friction both possible and effective. I refuse to accept the mere possibility of the Master lying or resorting to ancient potions in order to gain a full erectile reaction.[34]

The Abbot of Costello's Cathedral is more willing to accept that a mortal lie, or should we say a black lie, could have triggered the Master's bloodshot reaction. He claims that:

"What is done for the sake of humanity as a whole, travels far beyond the grasp of common judgement. What matters is the end, and He used part of his human-doll nature to achieve some amazing features in such stressful times for Him. Think, dear parishioners, if you could be able to achieve an effective circulation of the blood that would allow your *corpus cavernosum* to be

---

34 Nowadays, it is quite common to see how alternative therapies are being offered to those who refuse to ingest chemicals in order to regain the lost masculine potency. Mystical schools in which the adept is trained into different forms of Lies are blooming across the whole Western world (Ed.).

replenished during such a public and sombre situation. Ponder upon that."[35]

The discourse of Sir Rigobert Angus Buss continues like this:

> Under the light that this theory casts upon us, we can fully understand the reason why Pontius Pilatus washed his own hands at such a crucial moment in history; he was about to show the inexperienced wooden Messiah how to proceed with those adolescent feverish activities of selfish love. Even though he deserves all our eternal disdain, we should acknowledge, through our sense of chivalry, Pilatus' hygienic gesture of washing his hands before posing them on his private parts. Well done, Ponti!
>
> Naturally (and understandably), this theory has its adepts, its addicts, its inepts and those who are recovering from such a mess; but not only does this dialectical logical process offer us a much more sensible explanation about the wooden Messiah: in addition, it enlightens us in a matter of such importance as to what effectively was the *prima causa* that helped our Human Kind

---

35 It is worth emphasizing that Mark, the Abbot's Christian name, was a well-known mythomaniac, as well as a dexterous lover, whose fame extended throughout the hole of the British Empire (we can't be sure whether the absence of the letter w is deliberate or not – Ed.).

in the discovery of fire; without a doubt the milestone of our age, and the delight of chefs around the world.[36]

What about the resurrection?

In this case, we are inclined[37] to think that Pinocchio's *post mortem* appearance in the form of a flesh-and-blood being represents the victory of life over death, of light over shadows; flesh over wood, milk over my coffee and water over fire: the making of a complete Man.[38]

---

36 This simple historical fact could be used to explain some figures of speech such as *the fiery love passion, a passion like fire, the fire of love, you make me see fireworks, firecracker, we didn't start the fire, eternal flame, come on baby light my fire*, and those expressions that bond both Love and Fire in the same sentence. As the North American poet used to chant: "Love is the cause of Fire. Fire is the result of Love. O, tender and hardness dance together in the Genesis of Heat and Spit." We also give place to an awkward question such as: "What's the actual meaning of the song *Great Balls of Fire*?" Could it have something to do with this historical event? Does it represent the author's religious beliefs? Is the author an *avatar* of the Messiah? Fire, walk with me.

37 Could this be a hint of the author's sexual preferences and the posterior denouement of his life? (Ed.)

38 Thanks to the mathematical inquisitions performed by the great Russian polymath Sasha Romanenko, some left-wing churches are claiming what seems, at *prima facie*, to be a ridiculous assertion: "If the Messiah burned himself to death, then, his re-appearance into human form should be confined to the looks of a black man, or African American, or African British, or African Japanese, or African Asian American, and so forth, depending on where the church in question is based."

The ways of the Lord are inextricable, and so is the art of storytelling. In Pinocchio's biography, in Carlo Collodi's version, the Fairy Godmother is to be responsible for his ultimate transformation. According to words uttered by Sir Rigobert Buss's adjunct, the remarkable Abbot from Saint Chichastarmic Cathedral, Sir John Leigh Cab (only books in advance), the fantastic fairy-like character could have been inspired by Angel Gabriel's top-secret role in the Messiah's resurrection.

Does that imply that the Angel wore a fairy guise in order to distract the dying Messiah and to deceive Lucifer? Or was he, if we are allowed to give a gender to Mr Gabriel, really a fairy, who flew around with a magic wand? Did he (again, sorry for assuming a masculine naming) have a secret companion, *viz* the real fairy? And are fairies simply a re-adaptation of those angelic presences in the holy scriptures?

Thanks to some brilliant ideas, we are able to insinuate a possible explanation for this. What do we mean by *this*? Nobody knows, but nonetheless, we carry on with this exceptional speculatory piece of writing.

Regarding the Angel's Gabriel guise, Sir Rigobert Buss suggests that:

> There is nothing censurable about the Angel wearing a fairy costume; it is common knowledge that these angelic beings lack a proper gender (perhaps the *inventors* of gender fluidity?). It is perfectly natural for them to cross-dress, just as it's usual for a little chap in his late twenties to enjoy the overwhelming caresses of his mother's silk underwear over his scrotum as he plays football.

Nonetheless, we beg the reader not to panic in excess when confronted with this dialectical mayhem; these atrocious theories were completely unmasked and terminally discarded when the Vatican Secret Service found, both in Saint Chichastarmic Cathedral and at Sir Rigobert's private home, several thousand Pinocchio wooden dolls, along with stock shares of certain companies in the transportation business based in the West Indies and in New Delhi, of an estimated value of £7.8 billion, besides future estimates related to the selling boost of the infamous doll which – according to secret sources – was supposed to be launched into the market once the newest version of the New Testament had been altered and mass-distributed across the globe, with the sole greedy intention to embed the wooden Messiah as a central figure.

Such despicable human beings certainly do not deserve to be called *men*, not even *human beings*. So, we shall rephrase the last sentence:

Such despicable (...) certainly do not deserve to be called (...). They don't even deserve the benefit of being referred to as dolls.

In this case, we shall have to correct – yet again – the last written sentence:

Such despicable (...) do not certainly deserve to be called (...). They don't even deserve the benefit of being referred to as (...).

Honouring our coherence, we shall, for the last time, rephrase this assertion:

Such despicable do not certainly deserve to be called. They don't even deserve the benefit of being referred to as.

Finally, and making good use of what the former Sir Rigobert devised as a slogan, we do affirm that the ways of the Lord are indeed inextricable; and thankfully so.

A casual incident helped the public express their unanimous and categorical judgement (rejection), whose nature the reader shall soon easily understand; by the forces of chance – or fate, or perhaps it was the very own fate of chance, or a slight shadow of chance in fate itself – both former Sirs were seen at a public toilet in Hyde Park, putting into practice that reprehensible act of selfish and lavish love, with the help of their hands, and later, when the heat rose, with their mouths.[39]

According to newspaper reports of the time, in order to carry out that act of self-lust, they produced a complex machinery which seemed to represent a wooden arm, supposedly enacting the fake Pinocchio-Messiah's sacrificial act, whilst the other, immersed in the role of Pilatus, washed his hands frenetically and then taught the supposed wooden doll how to proceed accurately and carefully in the performing of such reprehensible act of self-love. A third masculine figure was spotted chanting and blowing kisses around the two excommunicated sinners, wearing an angelic guise whilst pretending to be Pinocchio's Fairy, all shrouded by the persistent smoke that was being offered by some little green twigs that were

---

39 Due to *decorum*, we cannot confirm whether the mouth was used for a selfish or altruistic act.

shyly burning in a corner, giving the horrendous rite a hellish ambience.[40]

---

40 A soon-to-be-known enormous number of deaths should be placed upon the shoulders of these creatures who, through their morbid and perverse theories, incited countless adolescents – and many who are well past that hardened stage – to fervently masturbate under the promise that they would experience the visit of the Holy Spirit, in the form of a crown made of fire. Drained of their seeds, with signs of starvation and dehydration, these innocent victims faced a fireless dry-death.

Ephemeris

On a sunny day like today,[41] though with a bit of cloud which gave the sun a timid countenance, in the distant and beautiful town of Nueva Palmira, the celebrated writer, humanist, composer, pianist (who played solely with his left hand despite having possession of a healthy and skilful right one, yet only when he was induced by the sour taste of several glasses of Espinillar), painter, lover of dragonfly fishing, lazy kisser and private detective, Radamés Washington "π" Funes Da Silva – who was also sometimes called simply 3.14 – died of a grave but indeed very grave accident.

The reader might question the lack of taste in referring to such a prodigy of nature by a mere number; why just 3.14?

The reason is fairly simple, and its origin is due to an innocent articulation which was uttered by a late humble mathematics teacher who by chance met our genius at the

---

41 It is believed that the above-mentioned day was the first day of the eighth month of 1876 (Ed.).

bar of the local *pulpería*; indeed both reason and origin would prove in the end to be deadly.

Perchance with a bit of modesty, whilst simultaneously demonstrating his love of numbers and calculations, Romualdo Giménez Ascasubi greeted the unsurpassed polymath with a bombastic salutation:

"*¿Cómo está mi admirado?* (How are you my admired) Radamés Washington 3.1415926535 8979323846

2643383279	5028841971	6939937510	5820974944
5923078164	0628620899	8628034825	3421170679
8214808651	3282306647	0938446095	5058223172
5359408128	4811174502	8410270193	8521105559
6446229489	5493038196	4428810975	6659334461
2847564823	3786783165	2712019091	4564856692
3460348610	4543266482	1339360726	0249141273
7245870066	0631558817	4881520920	9628292540
9171536436	7892590360	0113305305	4882046652
1384146951	9415116094	3305727036	5759591953
0921861173	8193261179	3105118548	0744623799
6274956735	1885752724	8912279381	8301194912
9833673362	4406566430	8602139494	6395224737
1907021798	6094370277	0539217176	2931767523
8467481846	7669405132	0005681271	4526356082
7785771342	7577896091	7363717872	1468440901
2249534301	4654958537	1050792279	6892589235
4201995611	2129021960	8640344181	5981362977
4771309960	5187072113	4999999837	2978049951
0597317328	1609631859	5024459455	3469083026
4252230825	3344685035	2619311881	7101000313
7838752886	5875332083	8142061717	7669147303
5982534904	2875546873	1159562863	8823537875

9375195778	1857780532	1712268066	1300192787
6611195909	2164201989	3809525720	1065485863
2788659361	5338182796	8230301952	0353018529
6899577362	2599413891	2497217752	8347913151
5574857242	4541506959... "		

Of course, by the time he reached the last recorded number, that mortal *nine*, Radamés Washington "π" Funes Da Silva had left the *pulpería* some fifty-seven days, eighty-six hours and seven thousand six hundred and thirty-six seconds before our late teacher could finally end his calculatory and remarkable reciting, and with it, his own life.[42]

It is worth remarking that "π" – or 3.14 – did not leave the place due to impoliteness or hardness of hearing; it is more than likely that, some minutes before the bombastic calculatory salutation had begun, don Radamés Washington "π" Funes Da Silva had wolfed down some juicy *chivitos*, bathed in his piquant vice in the form of tabasco, that went down his castigated digestive tract and inspired an unexpected series of intestinal clarion calls, thundering for immediate and necessary discharge action.

The *pulpería* had a precarious toilet whose indecent centre was a rotten and worm infested latrine; and given our hero's sitting preferences (some envious enemies used to call him *The*

---

42 Extreme autophagy, hypothermia, lack of oxygen, self-salival-drowning, starvation and boredom are some of the numerous possibilities considered by the local police regarding the cause of death. In some regions of the department of Colonia del Sacramento it is still debated whether he stopped reciting the numbers because of his unavoidable death, or whether he halted due to ignorance of the following figures and as a consequence only then did he expire, due to reasons that would eventually have to be explained if that possibility is to be confirmed.

King of Shit), he always preferred to exercise his own bowels within the realms of his private *finca*'s luxurious restrooms, in a controlled thus safe environment.[43]

It was for this reason only that our beloved Radamés never used to abandon his surroundings for more than a couple of weeks at a time; he had mastered and strengthened that muscular group called *Sphincter ani externus* to such an extent – elevating such contraction to a sublime artistic level – that he was not only able to withhold even the most challenging intestinal calls (except for spicy foods, which he tried to religiously avoid), but to perform amazing features with his very anus: open beer bottles, crack nuts, mould clay and other astonishing deeds; once, a teacher said during a physics class, paraphrasing Archimedes:

> "Give me the anus of Radamés, and I shall move the earth."[44]

---

43 He once rode his horse throughout the vast plains of Patagonia, during a seemingly endless forty-five days and without stopping once, in order to sit on his porcelain throne. The amazing features and hygienic standards of his restrooms forged the old Uruguayan saying: "It was so clean, that you could eat from his toilet."

44 Once confronted with this modest remembrance in the form of ephemeris, the famous Argentine psychiatrist Daniel Scianneus conjectured that our hero might have had some attachment problems, which therefore caused this extreme preference, probably originated after a filial abandonment, either by his mother, or by his father, or both, simultaneously or not; he also imagines that if 3.14 had ever decided to write an autobiography, in it he would have confessed that, for him, the act of defecating had a metaphorical meaning: that of giving birth to a new form of life, changed, transformed, transmuted, that eventually would feed another being, in a never-ending feasting chain that would lead to an infinite cycle of life and excrement.

Besides his eccentric toilet routines, he was a man of astonishing memory, being the first undocumented human being to reach 2.8 trillion digits after the common 3.14 – or π numbers – performing the amazing feature without writing down even a single number; but, alas, it was not enough: having achieved during an October afternoon such a mathematical exploit at the age of seven, something deep within, something that could not be evacuated through the force of will or the intestines, an idea – or an illusion – of perchance reaching that numerical end-point, kept silently haunting him ever since that ill-fated day of spring.

He always thought of Socrates as the exemplary Man; he was inspired by him along every breath he took after finding a tome, left by chance or a helping hand, at the very entrance of that same *pulpería* that was to become, some long years after, a witness of a famous bombastic mathematical salutation; a tome signed by a fellow named Plato.

After masticating the Socratic motto *Gnothi Seauton* or γνῶθι σεαυτόν for long enough, that is, till not even the last *n* was left to stand, bitten to dust, he decided that someone who was ignorant of his own full name was incapable of commencing the Delphic journey towards self-knowledge.

This thirst for knowledge threw him into a frantic study of his own written denominational nature; but he knew (a knowledge swiftly masked by his greed, the greed that is all-disguising and all-concealing), before embarking on such a quest, that he was doomed from the beginning: his own name was infinite and eternal, as the Universe, as the God with ninety-nine faces. He once wrote:

If I could have had the chance to completely embrace my name, to fully know myself, I would have become that exemplary Man; One who transcends the vastness of Mathematical conjurations; One that would have become God, thus mastering and performing his ninety-nine shapes and absorbing the vibration of the hundredth secret name.

This dreadful and unsuccessful quest, along with the incredible trials and tribulations suffered due to his lavatorial preferences, left him little time for other mundane activities; nonetheless, he will also be remembered as the lifelong and truthful friend of Abu Kasem – from whom he learned everything he knew about perfumes and alchemy – as well as a dear collaborator that helped the Greedy Perfumer's *Opus Magnum* manifest in this dimension.

The last divine numbers prefigured and calculated by his unique mind were (and are) 7 8 6.

This commitment to the Socratic *motto* and his unquenchable thirst for knowledge made him embark on a journey that he knew from the beginning would be life-threatening, and perhaps deadly: the prospect of having to endure several weeks, probably months, without being able to lighten himself of unnecessary baggage was, to say the least, challenging, if not insane.

Rumours drew him to the Atacama desert, a vastness where nothing reigns but the monotonous sand, and whatever dares to exist is doomed to an atrocious struggle for survival. Radamés was convinced that in those mortal sands there was a clue destined to be found; a key to unlock the mystery of his endless name, a key that would provide him a passage to immortality.

His strategy (and challenge), from the very beginning of the expedition, was to eat the minimum amount of food and drink only the necessary water in order to not wake those intestines that – inevitably and slowly – were beginning to get packed like the Tokyo subway during rush hour.

After three hellish months of barely urinating and constant perineum compressions, of having lost his three *compañeros* and having eaten his horses in homeopathic doses, he finally understood – perhaps fate forced him to do so – that he was wrong: "The end of that which is infinite cannot be reached, but only experienced through earthly existence. Live your precious life, man, and get home before your bowels explode!"

Those wise words, uttered with a tone of disdain by a wandering dervish, proved in the end to be decisive; without having lost an ounce of weight, yet gaining instead several kilos of crammed waste waiting to be expelled like the seed of a virgin male arriving at his forties, at first he tried to jump on the back of his lovely *yegua criolla plateada*; yet, unfortunately, not only was she unable to bear that amount of extra luggage that her master stubbornly carried within, but 3.14 was incapable of lifting his own weight.

After taking advantage of the intuition of the animal, which laid herself down *camel-style* after finding herself bathed in her master's sweat, Radamés was ready to go back and lovingly embrace, once again, his holy toilet grail.

The journey home was slower than expected, and the constant yet painful gallop proved to be fatal for his withholding mission;[45] the problem had already started to internally spread during the third evening of the ride, and our ill-fated hero not only had an intestinal system that was already working far beyond its actual capacity, but the excrements were slowly invading the neighbouring organ-realms: the liver, the spleen, and according to rumours they were planning to take on the pancreas.

His body had already become a chessboard invaded by the enemy's (his own) army, yet all tainted brown and foul smelling.

After trials and tribulations experienced (suffered) throughout a pilgrimage to his evacuatory throne that lasted generous weeks abundant in sweat, chills and nightmares – both during his vigil and his slumber – which tempted him with porcelain grails that were barely worthy for the infidels and insulting to his own creed (or with silky smooth bushes and even the barren sand of the desert), it was only his spirit which was strengthened when the fragrant presence of eucalyptus in the air announcing the vicinity to his *axis mundi* woke him up; his body was about to burst in faeces.

The beautiful mare – exhausted – abandoned him a few miles from the main farmhouse; walking wearily whilst carrying twice the amount of his natural weight, Radamés felt that his heart was refusing to give in, thus providing the

---

45 The conundrum seems, even today, hellish: to ease the pace and risk the strength of the anal gates preventing the flood; or to hasten it yet let the movement act as the chant of the mermaids.

necessary inspiration and encouragement to his lungs, that were on the verge of being flooded with his own excrement, accumulated throughout months of withholding his posterior discharge during an impossible expedition that might have been doomed from its beginning.

He was at the threshold of his domain.

As his feverish mind continued to calculate the extension of his numerical name (something which he never ceased to ponder and seek while he was alive... even during the ordeal he chose to suffer out of respect for his defecatory creed) to finally arrive at the hindmost figure – the number 6 – with an unfamiliar taste invading his tongue and the reflection of his porcelain throne blessing those eyes that had never stopped searching, his own Anal Grail, Radamés Washington "π" Funes Da Silva... expired.

His influence might have reached the shores of Jorge Luis Borges by inspiring his masterly *Funes the Memorious*.

Also, four hundred and fifty-seven years, thirty-four months, fifteen hours and nineteen seconds ago, in the French region of Lorraine, it rained.

Sentence

"You will be what you must be, or else you will be nothing."

José Francisco de San Martín Gómez y Matorras, better known as José de San Martín, after a couple of glasses of cognac in a tavern of dubious reputation, located in the Quartier Latin du Paris.

Proverb

"He who knows not, and knows not that he knows not, is a fool; shun him.

He who knows not, and knows that he knows not, is a child; teach him.

He who knows, and knows not that he knows, is asleep; wake him.

But he who knows, and knows that he knows, is a sage; follow him."

Ancient Arab proverb

Justice

A big debate is under way – and indeed it is fair to admit that it is already really far, far, far away – ignited by the lines published in the Israeli tabloid *Shlalom*, dedicated to the famous crossover tenor, André Bobassi, who is recognized worldwide for his several hits such as "I Crave for Your Sweat"; "I Sweat to God"; "Baby, I Sweat to You It's True"; and "All You Need is Sweat".

He is also known to have been born blind.

Despite his mother's attempts to force him into the literary world – encouraged by the hope (and fear as well, because both are inseparable) of raising a future Milton or Borges – the young veiled man was at a young age seduced (though some critics deduce that given his poor musical gifts, to think of it in terms of a seduction does sound petty; yet the possibility that he could have been abused repeatedly, and maybe even humiliated by means of sadomasochism does not) by the chant of the nine daughters of Zeus; it was this Greek vocalise which in the end determined that music was to be his own Fate and Destiny... and our very doom.

This is precisely the subject touched, circumcised and licked (and a bit more, according to different sources) by *Shlalom*'s Sunday edition:

> …It is for these reasons – and some other ones – that we have firm evidence to believe, and then take a step forward and assert that the Maestro André Bobassi is not blind. Sources within the music industry have assured this same journalistic Olympus that his now uncovered *fake* blindness is nothing but a vile and greedy stratagem perpetrated by his management team, designed and crafted to help overcome and conceal André's more than poor vocal condition and non-existent technical skills.
>
> Once his handicapped condition had been installed in the subconsciousness of the masses, that divine trinity represented by those human feelings of compassion, pity and mercy would transform that flock of probable consumers into an easy prey of the capitalist world incarnated, or better said, disguised in those garments of the music industry.
>
> Those same lifesaving and maybe instinctive feelings would ultimately be manipulated to make the poor fake-blind-almost-singer succeed; a voiceless fraud that became an all-audience romantic extravagant and sweaty product.

The above-mentioned lines served as an unstoppable inspiration for Professor Christian Rigobund Pyke, head, armpit, leg and *Alma pater* of the psychology department of the University of Salamanca, to organize a symposium about Ethics, Journalism and Arts. He is going to be accompanied by Maestro John Pi at the Piano – though he is not supposed to play at all times, unless things become quite unbearable – and also by a panel of distinguished scientists, artists, footballers, pimps, sweaty priests, speculators, sophists and naturally, the host and moderator of such a breathtaking event, the world famous and celebrated art critic, connoisseur of the operatic world and *bon vivant*, Mr Jonas Arklingdon.

We now proceed to transcribe the exact content of the symposium.[46]

Jonas Arklingdon: Hello, and welcome to this live conference about journalism boundaries, blindness, art and marketing. Let me introduce to you our wonderful panel of guests here today, whom I deeply thank for joining us for such a marvellous display of human intelligence. Doctor, PhD, and Professor from the Saint Andrews of the Hills University, Mr Dev Grandashenak.

(Professor Pyke is getting up off his seat and approaches the dais. John Pi commences to caress the first notes of *Für Elise*, as the *Alma pater* seems to be making some remarks to Mr Jonas about the opening speech. He quietly returns to his pompous armchair, as Pi stops on the fourth bar)

---

46 For a better understanding and appreciation of what now has entered the annals of scholastic history, we suggest that the symposium ought to be read out loud, if possible, in the key of G major.

Mr Jonas Arklingdon absorbs the sweat that bathes his forehead with a white handkerchief and after a hard swallow, re-commences:

JA: Hello Ladies, Gentlemen, and Sweaty ill-fated human beings. I now have the honour of opening our symposium about Ethics, Journalism, Blindness, Art and Marketing. It is my pleasure to introduce you, one by one of course, otherwise it could be terribly painful (a few intuitive giggles can be perceived in the lecture room) unless you have a sweaty ugly posterior orifice (now the giggles become a mix of spits, booing and uncontrollable laughs, as Professor Pyke ingests fifty-six Valiums and John Pi plays Berio's *Sequenza IV* at a frenetic speed). In the first place, I extend my gratefulness to all of you here present tonight. Now, without further ado, I shall present the lecturers.

(In the typical fake voice of radio announcers everywhere)

In the blue corner, weighing three hundred fifty pounds, with an astonishing record of three hundred sixty symposiums absorbed by his ears, never defeated in a face-to-face debate, and never spat a single drop of saliva during a sophistic challenge, the amazing and dialectical Doctor, PhD and Professor from the Saint Andrews of the Hills University, Mr Dev Grandashenak!!!

(John Pi improvises some chords that are supposed to sound something like *Eye of the Tiger*, from *Rocky IV*, but his sweaty fingers make his playing extremely difficult and chord sequence impossible to identify for the great audience)

Dev Grandashenak: Hello Jonas.

JA: Hello Professor... is it true that you are a great cook?

DG: Well, that depends mainly on the outside temperature, or if my pants are wet, or if you take a look at my *cook* just after I left the pool; let me check now... (he begins to unfasten his belt)

(John Pi dries his fingers, taking advantage of his hairy legs, and suggests the melody of Joe Cocker's *You Can Leave Your Hat On*)

JA: I think you misunderstood me, (raising his voice a little more) is it true that you are a great **cook**?

DG: Oh! Sorry (he blushes and vomits). Yes, am I.

JA: Sorry to correct you my dear friend, but you should say *Yes, I am*.

DG: You are wrong! Am I, not you!

JA: Sorry, you seem not to understand my point; when I say *I am*, I'm simply implying that *you* are the great cook.

DG: Are you trying to say that you are me, and I am you? Let me check (again, he unfastens his belt and starts to lower his trousers, but the host rapidly saves him from further shame).

(John Pi attempts to play a chord, but his hands slip from the keyboard and his front teeth play their first and last two notes of their lives; he bleeds profusely as the white keyboard becomes red)

JA: There's no need to perform a trouserless debate my dear friend...

DG: So, if you are me, who the hell I am?

JA: It's *I am* for fuck's sake! It's fairly simple: you are Professor, PhD, etc., etc., Dev Grandashenak, and I am Jonas.

DG: OK, but if you want to be me, at least give me – you – your name and that wonderful tie you – am I – are wearing (for those readers who might ignore the kind of tie Jonas is wearing, it's a silk violet one, bought in Cartier, and by the way matches those mystical green eyes of his).

JA: No, please Doctor, I would not even pretend to be such a genius as you are.

DG: Who is the genius here, you, am I, you are, are you, or I am?

JA: You are, Professor, of course, *you are*. Am I right? (He asks the audience)

(The crowd roars a huge *affirmative* chant in D major, while pianist John Pi tries some sweat wristbands on and biting a cotton cloud in order to stop the profuse bloody tears his gums are producing after bidding farewell to those couple of deceased little white keys, called teeth)

DG: OK then, *are* you!

JA: No professor, *you* are!

DG: Oh, I see now (epiphany face as Handel's Hallelujah is suggested by Pi's piano). I am! Thanks for the compliment Jonas. You are a wonderful critic as well.

JA: I feel really flattered dearest Dev (he seems to be indeed very fond of Grandashenak).

Third unannounced and quite anxious panellist: "Please, could you carry on with the symposium please?"

JA: Are you jealous, you sweaty bitch?

(John Pi goes to the pharmacy to get more Valium for Professor Pyke, who has just run out of pills, and leaves a trace of sweat and blood on his way out)

Third unannounced panellist again, even more anxious than before: "Come on! How can you imply such a thing? He is not my type at all!"

JA (after receiving serial warnings from a Valium-infested Professor Pyke): Sorry beloved audience, we continue thus, presenting our next guest. She is a wonderful pedagogue, philosopher and visiting professor at the Ontario College of Advanced Religious and Philosophical Studies. Please welcome Professor Julia Huthensrothengerber.

JH: Hello Jonas. Love your tie.

(Possibly because Julia Huthensrothengerber is actually *the* most influential scholar and *the* chicest intellectual erudite of the religious scholastic scene, some members of the audience appear to be confused as to whether they would physically love their ties, or only in a platonic manner. I can spot some men trying to squeeze their silky ties under their pants; from where I sit, I cannot be sure whether they try to rub them against their masculine tool, or to insert the garment where it's not supposed to be worn. Others start to lick them, kiss them, as they attempt to share their ties with other men's wives. All different types of orgies start to take place, but I can also see that a group is just pleasuring themselves as they admire their neckties. The Plato adepts simply compose odes and poems for those admired and beloved ideal forms that mortals call *ties*, which are placed over silky cushions, as they chant their way around John Pi's piano, who, by a stroke of luck, is wearing a dinner jacket. Mayhem of ethereal and explicit love manifestations inundates the classroom for some passionate minutes. The stench of sweat and its vapours can be felt in the air; also some dairy perfume can be smelt)

Things start to calm down after the *Alma pater* of the symposium chambers his Magnum .45, whilst attempting to swallow a mouthful of Valiums.

JA: Come again please? (Still quite altered and distracted by the previous quarrel, he uses his tie to dry his damp forehead)

JH: I'm afraid nature has imposed over my physical body some other limitations in addition to my sweaty bottom... I'm not multi-orgasmic.

(General mocking laugh, whilst some exhausted lovers are smoking with their ties around their heads and some pizza delivery men carry vast boxes of pizzas around the cloister; also, some ties are being dispatched in taxis to unknown destinations)

Doctor Dev approaches Professor Julia Huthensrothengerber's seat and comforts her. Then he speaks.

DG: That's not something to be afraid of, darling. Let me show you how it's supposed to be done... (He desperately tries to unbutton his trousers, forgetting the belt strangling his greasy fat abdomen. Some security personnel force some Valiums down his throat, and slap him in the face. Now he seems to have calmed down, sitting in his place as he zips up his fly)

JA (who by the way seems to be a nerve-wreck, his attempts to dry his sweaty cascade is useless; his tie is already soaking wet and unsuitable to prevent the salty rain from burning his eyes): And finally, our last guest for today, the emeritus Bishop of Angsburg, Johann von Gettrewerktschiterassden. Thank you, Father, for coming.

Johann von Gettrewerktschiterassden: Holy Ghost! Can you tell? I thought the stain was unnoticeable! It's Shakespeare all over again!

JA: That's not what I mean, Father! I was only thanking you for attending the symposium, of course.

JvG: I'm not your father at all! That can't be possible. I swear to God that I did use a condom and then fed my cat with what was left in it!

JA: Pardon me, but I was not implying any sort of blood bond, only a figurative way of calling you a spiritual father.

JvG: Well, but I have never met you, so I could have had no influence on you!

JA: Sorry Father, but I don't mean that for real. It's just a respectful way of addressing you.

JvG: I see. But let me inform both you and the audience, that you are expected to call me *Your Excellency*, or Bishop von Gettrewerktschiterassden at the very least!

JA: Sorry *not* Father, but *Your Excellency*. Moving on towards what's important and the reason why we are here tonight, I shall then reveal the questions-conundrums that have inspired this meeting right now.

Is André Bobassi really blind? Is it possible *not* to be born blind, and then, by a marketing manoeuvre, become so? Is it humanly feasible? Is that the so-called divine trilogy, incarnated into pity, mercy and compassion, capable of destroying the true and transcendent artistic perception?

Is it accepted by the eye of the Church? How many eyes does the Church have? Can the Church be blind?[47]

Professor Dev Grandashenak: As a man of science, I will begin by naming some of the different possibilities that should be considered:

- He was born blind
- He became blind due to accident or health failure
- He was born blind, because his immortal soul knew beforehand that his voice was not going to be fit for such operatic endeavours; this is the reason why his wise *anima*, let's say, *chose* to be born blind in order to learn and succeed, thus overcoming all limitations
- He was fond of Stevie Wonder and José Feliciano, so in wanting to be like them, deprived himself of his visual sense through the all-conquering power of desire and emotional greed
- His marketing agency, perpetrating a macabre plan, inflicted that deficiency only because of greed
- He... (interrupted by moderator)

JA: Thank you, Professor. We perfectly see your point, and we are really happy to be able to *see* it (as he winks towards the audience, who now laugh hysterically). So, what do the rest of you think?

---

47 Carrying that question further, yet not too much otherwise it would become impossible to be seen, is it possible to imagine that such a lack of vision by the Church is the cause of so much fondling and abuse of innocent children across the globe, and the subsequent impunity enjoyed by the highest ranks of the religious institution?

(Professor Grandashenak exits the conference quite upset, still trying to loosen his belt, but because he is so focused on finally getting rid of his trousers, fails to notice the sweaty-bloody stain previously produced by John Pi – a.k.a. cotton biter – and fatally slips, breaking his neck)

JH: Fake. He sings horribly and his blindness is nothing but a charade to move his audience into a chaos of pity and greedy sympathy; the *motto* that every salesman knows: If you cannot sell through word and charm, resort to the long arms of pity.

JvG: I can't think of the human race in those despicable terms. I'm sure he embraced his fate in a heroic way, thus inspiring the rest of us mere mortals to drink from the unending fountains of hope and greed.

JA: Come again Excellency?

JvG: Later darling, when we are alone. Naughty Jonas. (He blows a kiss directed at the moderator)

(At this very moment, John Pi imitates the sound of a sexy-sounding sax with his lips, as he improvises – not without utter difficulty – some porn chords on the keyboard that now appears to be floating due to the vast amounts of sweat that the moderator is exuding, mixed with some sticky remains from the orgiastic tie feast)

JA (visibly ashamed and almost drowning in his own sweat): Well, let me read to you all a letter from his management headquarters in Zürich, that has been faxed to us some minutes ago. It reads:

(An unknown gentleman from the audience insists in knowing precisely how many minutes ago the fax arrived. He is forced to swallow some Valium pills as he shouts about his right to know the precise figure)

JA continues his reading: "No comments". But, on the other hand, I have another letter from his fan club that says:

(Interrupted again by another unknown gentleman of the audience)

Unknown Gentleman: You don't have that fan club letter in your other hand. How many hands you've got mate? You got the fax on your left, and your right hand is holding that big...

(At that very moment, a security guard knocks the unknown-not-so-gentleman down, and leaves a tablet of Valium by his side; John Pi accompanies, fluttering and gasping for air, the brutality with some Nino Rota tunes)

Again, almost dehydrated and with his three piece suit soaked in sweat, Mr Jonas Arklingdon continues: How can anyone imagine or simply consider that such a reprehensible scheme could be perpetrated in order to sell 189.546.546.135.465.795,8 albums? It is outrageous! Nevertheless, the best testimony by far...

(Again, interrupted by a man who claims he is related to the knocked-down not-so-gentleman-and-intoxicated-with-Valium chap)

Unknown Gentleman II: How far?

JA: As far as a chicken can travel without the weight of three eggs in her interior.

(The answer appears to somehow have puzzled the now silent and calculating questioner)

JA: As I was saying, the best testimony, naturally, is that from the artist himself. Yes, André Bobassi wrote a letter that appeared today in the early edition of the *New York Hourglass*. The only problem that the editorial staff of the prestigious newspaper encountered was whether to publish or not what was supposed to be a letter (thus termed after the envelope that contained it); the handwriting was very poor, almost illegible, as if it had been written by, indeed, a blind man. They decided to contact the singer himself, who after being talked into appreciating the advantages of publishing a letter that could be read and understood, decided to dictate another one to his personal assistant and secretary:

"I'm destroyed. In these times, where conspiracy theories are the *crème de la crème*, I decided to fight for my honour and artistic integrity. I'm not a fake or self-inflicted blind man. I assure you that my life is a torture. I am one of the wealthiest men alive, yet unable to see, watch and enjoy through my eyes all that money can buy; not able to savour the massive profits that *you*, dear fans, enable me to earn. Torturous.

"You might say that I should be able to enjoy trips. Impossible. A horrible waste of time. Pyramids are being described to me as if I could somehow imagine what the fuck they are talking about; they even try to make some replicas, pretending those great Egyptians once were dwarfs, so I can feel them with my own hands; but still, I am not amazed to sense a sandcastle done by a dexterous little kid. The hanging gardens of Babylon, whose depictions I cannot understand even in Braille. The Chinese wall; the Fuji volcano, home of the immortal Koji Kabuto; they are nothing but words from a soulless tourist guide who only wants my money, and probably my girls.

"Though true it is, beloved reader, respected detractor: exceedingly difficult proved to be the finding of the system that now allows me, once and for all, to know if my feminine entourage is at her ripe point, be it for not breaking the law, be it for not swimming in Oedipal waters; the monthly reddish tasting is infallible.

"Now, going back to the travel issues: breathtaking dawns are being narrated to me from the luxurious balconies of the world's most exclusive hotels, and I can't see shit. The hottest babes die for me (of course, not in a Shakespearean way),[48] and I can barely imagine what a breast might look like. I'm always being admired for my cars, in which I'm usually driven around, but I've got no fucking clue what you are talking about mate! I can only feel that something is moving, and the same voice that asks: '*Come stai* André?'

"I can only talk in favour of food, something that really turns me on, in all the possible ways you can imagine; and yes, food makes me also die in *that* Shakespearean way as well. It adds some texture and taste of my liking. The only negative side to it is that sometimes, every now and then, some son of a crazy vicious bitch puts a bug in my dish; I suspect Stevie might be to blame. Usually, it's too late when I realize that what I'm about to swallow is not *penne al pesto*.

"So, dear detractors, dearest fans: don't envy me, don't haunt me; the capitalist world is made for those who can see, and I can't see shit. My only hope lies in finding Pinocchio, for He is the chosen one, and will surely be keen to help me. O my wooden Messiah,[49] make me your Bartimaeus!

---

48 See: Consufion
49 See: Final Debate

"With my heart. André Bobassi."

JA: Shame is what made all the experts abandon the premises, and left me all alone, sweaty and in tears. In fact, I can't say if it's the sweat that's flooding my eyes, or those emotional tears that were inspired by such a profound statement.

(A postman rapidly enters the scene, trying not to be tempted by the enormous quantities of Valium floating about, and swims towards the atrium and carefully handles Mr Jonas Arklingdon a telegram. Later realizing that he is swimming in sweat, the postman starts vomiting and dies because of it)

JA (spitting sweat since it's starting to enter his mouth as his breathing is becoming more spacious given the amount of mucus accumulated in the nose area): But I have some breaking news to share. A cable just arrived, and the *Rottersburgers Tageblatt* is planning to publish in its very late night edition, the following news:

(Almost panting and about to faint, trying to cling to the atrium, as the rest of the audience struggles to keep afloat. I can barely hear the aquatic music that John Pi is attempting... surely a piano version of Water Music)

"The famous possibly blind tenor – though not operatic and barely pop – philanthropist and former swimming pool cleaner André Bobassi, could have donated his entire fortune estimated at 7.9 trillion euros to a mysterious foundation whose secret and infamous objective would be that of driving all the blind millionaires of the world into bankruptcy. The façade is perfect and commendable, but the real intentions are not so pure. All the funds collected are deposited in a secret bank account at a secret bank in a top-secret island that lies between two other ultra-secret islands. Once the information is exposed, the secret becomes bigger and turns out to be an ultra-super-infinite secret. As far as we know, there could be approximately 3.7 billion secretive levels that separate us from the main question: What happens with all the money that comes from the former billionaires?

"An inside informer is able to confirm that the foundation's motto is *to free all the blind humans from the flagellum of also being millionaires or billionaires*. The name of such an institution is, due to its super-duper secretive status, rumoured to be Happy but Poor Blind Fellows, and his honorary president, the unscrupulous not-so-blind and former Stevie Wonder tour manager, Mr Slavos Miroslav Espinoza, who was born in Hungary but later adopted Ecuadorian nationality simply because he wanted to. Others say it was his love for bananas and Delfín Quishpe's music that motivated him to adopt the condored[50] South American flag. Espinoza recently pointed out in a secret interview given to a secret reporter who works for a secret magazine that: *to be blind and millionaire or billionaire, is like being punished with a penalty and a red card for the same foul; we all know that suffering a double punishment for a single deed is not fair. It's against common sense!*"

(About to die, pale and almost without pulse, floating about the atrium, Jonas Arklingdon continues with the last remaining air that his lungs will ever taste)

---

50 The flag of Ecuador features the splendorous presence of this carnivorous bird.

JA: André Bobassi's whereabouts are a mystery, but some rumours indicate that he might be living a thundery and passionate romance with Pinocchio; whereas other gossip whisperers assert that they are only friends, they together attempt to give light to a certain social movement that, according to ultra-top-mighty-super-duper-tupper-moped-exclusive sources, will shake and burn the world down to resurrective ashes. The latest set of rumours indicates that the last couple of rumours are rubbish, and that this whole symposium and pseudo-humorous account is not funny at all. But what we do know for certain is that the lovely (now doubtful or suspected) couple might also be considering building an extra bedroom in their simple cottage, with a complex fire alarm system, located in the suburbs of Lyon.[51] But the question still remains unanswered: is this only a rumour, a part of an untold piece of gossip, or simply a mere unrealised possibility floating about the waters of infinite probabilities?

Shortly after pronouncing the word probabilities, though it really sounded like *lfndfdjdfhkdfjsties*, Mr Jonas Arklingdon died of dehydration, paradoxically, floating in his own sweat.

Moments after, Professor Christian Rigobund Pyke, revealing a super-human resistance to Valium, broke wind and ate a ripe banana as he floatingly exited the

---

51 Some claim to have seen the former superstar singer, walking without any aid whatsoever, and jumping happily on the streets. On the other hand (the right one) we have those who are sure that they have seen the in-love André, wearing dark glasses, during a grey and typical English day. Others claim that the stone-baked pizza is the best.

sweating-pool-room, leaving behind him some nasty bubbles. He and the Maestro Pi used the piano as a lifesaving-floating device.

The man who served as *observer*, that is, contributing all those words between (), died as well, just like every remaining person of the audience, due to the toxic smell provided by such a mixture of both non-sticky and sticky liquids.

The two front teeth of the Maestro Pi are still to be found.

The Wayfarer

The wayfarer who retraces the path of the tradition, walks on a sword, perhaps infinite.

A curved sword that emerges from multitudes, melting into one.

The wayfarer walks in a constant (dis)equilibrium, oscillating between hell and paradise; between happiness and sadness; punishment or reward: fictions.

There are only two real punishments: inaction when facing an unveiled truth, and forgetfulness.

The executioner has your own name and is anxiously awaiting...

The wayfarer of the tradition walks in search of the only real state: the presence over the impeccable edge.

Blame

The mistake is the potential for learning
Error is the unrecognized lesson
Stupidity is not doing what one knows needs to be done
Sin is to not hit the target... which is oneself
Horror is the forgetfulness of all the above

Opprobrium

The following is a precise depiction of a moment endured by the human race in a recent past.

The famous religious tabloid *Il Corriere della Piazza Popolare Vaticana* published these surprising lines:

_____
_____
_____
_____
_____
_____.

I'm afraid *that* was a little harmless joke. Here are the *real* lines, which by the way have nothing to do with the Nazca lines:

From within the highest ranks of the Vatican, which include our most honourable and beautiful Pope Francesco XPFJDHSLGHB, those eternal and concealed all-powerful and all-knowledgeable behind-the-curtain

Cardinals, a weird wooden puppet, a supposedly blind[52] crossover singer and a young lady whose dress is still showing the side effects of lap dying,[53] an official document has been recently released in which the greatest and most humble Pope ever states that the actual ban on naming gay priests will be applied in a retroactive manner. This means that all priests ordained *after* the second day of the year 1910 of our Lord are expected not to have expressed in the accountable past – nor to actually express in the actual present – any sort of signal of longing or of physical manifestation of love towards a congener: which is to say, no human being of the masculine gender who has had, might have or shall have, a virile member that in appearance is similar to the aforementioned cleric."

Naturally – as it was to be expected – this has created a quite bombastic agitation within the belly of the Vatican; a great cloud of concern is floating (with a 98% chance of strong showers and winds) above the ruling elite of the Holy City, as well as over some local dioceses which are already desperately seeking future **manly** priests in order to prevent a long-feared – and perhaps foreseen – lack of God's workers.

The religious club is losing members, and the Islamic and barbaric foe must be outnumbered at any cost;

---

52 See: Justice
53 See: Similarities

such is the attitude being reinforced in every Catholic church – and in the "liberal" discourse forged in higher spheres and disguised as genuine concern for the health of the Imperialistic West – worldwide; though we are allowed to ask whether that shortage of members might have something to do with the fondness shown by some important leading figures in the ecclesiastical ranks – and the rings conformed by the powerful elite – towards certain inappropriate *members*... innocent, vulnerable and underaged?

This is a surprise to many,[54] and not quite a novelty for others.

Some studies affirm that if this ban were to be applied in this precise second – the 49th of the hour – or during this precise moment (though it is worth emphasizing that *this* is already a bit further away than the past 49th second of the *still* same hour), being *now* the third hour of the eighth day of the seventh month of a...,[55] the Church would only have five 100% old-fashioned and assured male priests

---

54 Is it fair to ask how many? Yes, it is (Ed.). Loose footnote: OK then, how many? According to last polls, many imply around 1.3 trillion people. Following loose footnote: And Others? A poll is under way. Results will be published as soon as possible. Almost last inquiring footnote: *ad aeternum ad imaginatus.* Last explanatory footnote: Implies that the joke could go on eternally, provided your imagination can create those proper conditions for humour to grow *ad aeternum ad imaginatus.*

55 Due to both security reasons and the deplorable state in which the original text is, we can't explicitly state the year. Among other reasons, because we, those responsible for these lines, do not consider it safe or appropriate to expose a date to uncertain abuses, by making it explicit.

left,[56] and other three whose culinary preferences – which have nothing to do with food – are under suspicion; of course, this is only counting those servants of God who are still (biologically) alive.

This last suspected *trio* are being submitted to certain screenings of different types of films that are quite popular within the homosexual community, as well as theatrical plays and musicals, in order to measure both the reactions of their neural-transmission network and the physical responses that could occur when, for instance, Julia Roberts gets the chance to buy all the dresses she fancies in the modern pro-prostitution adaptation of *Cinderella*.

Besides this test of psychological endurance, the suspected *trio* will be subsequently submitted to endless sodomy sessions in which several Pinocchio dolls of different sizes and shapes, such as the overweight Pinocchio, Basketball Centre Pinocchio, Rugby Prop Pinocchio, Bulimic Pinocchio, and the predictable *ad libitum ad aeternum*, will be introduced through the spot that *shan't ever be caressed by the warming thus drying rays of the sun*, as a poet would sing it.

---

56 It appears to be a flagrant oxymoron, given that not a single human being can claim to be a 100% heterosexual. The human nature is formed of Yin and Yang vibrations, both energetic flows coexisting within one body, though not within one steady self; thus states Dr Richard Gamblemasterputty, emeritus professor of the *Max Planck Institute for the Better Understanding of the Human Spices*. Yes, it is *correctly* written: *Spices*.

The predictable – and at this stage obvious – aim is to confirm or discard the supposed homosexual aberration;[57] if the suspected *trio* refuses to play in a childish manner with those wooden dolls that shall soon switch races (they are expected to become a bit more mixed-skinned rather than pure Caucasians after the posterior visits), the result will be as clear as the waters of the Ganges.

Bets in the Indonesian markets pay 5/10 in favour of the suspected deviation.[58]

The new chosen postulates or candidates, if elected and if there are indeed any, will be paid a generous wage (secret sources suggest an eight-figure monthly salary), including two-month paid vacation and also, as a compliment of the

---

57 Manfred Alt, famous libertarian and psychiatrist of the Jungian School, objects: *It is not the act itself that defines the sexual preference, but that intimate attraction felt by the adorer or the perceiver. It does not matter what you do, but what you long for.* Or as Pluto, also known as Plato's cousin, would have put it into words: *Thou art what Thou long for.*

58 The reader can, at this stage and due to the lack of further clarification, feel free to assume that all those who rank higher than priests are not affected by this new prohibition. Famous constitutionalist and world-celebrated barrister Dr John Parrish expressed some concerns in a letter published in *The Times*, Sunday edition. It reads: *That which is not forbidden, is assumed to be allowed. Must I assume, as a proud member of the Catholic Church, that those called, for instance, Abbots, are free to choose between an orange, a marmot, a capybara, a goat, a man or a woman?* After reading such a letter we can perfectly understand why former Dr, now simply John Parrish, was expelled from the London College of Law. He got the reply he deserved through the pen of an unknown reader of *The Times*, which was published the following Sunday: *It's obvious that the Abbots have dedicated their entire lives and have sworn to serve God beyond any carnal temptation. You should be ashamed to call yourself a 'proud member of the Catholic Church', fuck off.*

house, free access to a vast variety of prostitutes, including the favourites of the ruling political elite; we are informed that all girls **are of legal age**.

The tests that these aspirants must face are suspected to be, according to some rumours, utterly difficult; according to some other rumours, tremendously difficult. Here are some examples:

- A wild weekend with Pinocchio and the world-famous singer André Bobassi
- Reading Abu Kasem's *Opus Magnum* for seventy-five days in a row without eating or drinking
- And some other very difficult tasks which, due to lack of creativity and the roasting Moroccan heat, will not be explicated in this report[59]

What will happen with those nuns of the opposite sex, that which is female?

What will occur with the Yin force within the Vatican?

A group of nuns, represented by Sister Roina van der Strajkglksjnfjkfhsdndun, head, arm and legs of the Dutch Carmelites, expressed some concerns about the actual mayhem into which the institution is falling; she is not only worried about those dubious testing methods' ethics, but also about the risks of serious injury that the Church itself is running by falling in such a manner.

These disturbed feminine holy workers, in light of what happened with their priest brothers, wonder if they

---

59 Temperature seems to have fallen to 21° Celsius, but I'm not in the mood. Sorry.

could ever, through an overly intense affective inclination, commit themselves to love other women in a physical or mental fashion; and they also raised a question that has been haunting those ill-fated divine workers for centuries: can a woman with a moustache – or the foreshadowing of one – still be considered a woman?

The reply came swiftly but not without the much-expected element of surprise; it was shocking and revolutionary as well. Dictated to one of his favourite *gentiluomi* by the Pope himself, it reads:

> Dearest sisters, you can freely choose from the human menu available at life's diner. The only requirement is that we, Pope, Patriarchs, Major Archbishops, Cardinals, Primates, Metropolitans, Archbishops, Diocesans Bishops, and every servant that ranks higher than priesthood, must be able to watch at all times and in all places those delights of your love endeavours; it makes no difference to us if a man, several men, a woman or several of them, a cow, a whole herd of them, or even sheep, are involved; we shall not even complain about the number of participants in that delicious and sinful stew, nor if you practise by yourselves the arts of selfish love. Dear sisters, you choose what is of your fancy, and we will be watching, unnoticed. And yes, you are still a woman even if that feeble moustache shadows your mouth from the north.

PS: This lack of boundaries carries naturally some petite requests on our part. You are to share your make-up, underwear and diet tips with us.

Finis.

Predictably, the above-mentioned letter inspired passionate debates around the religious world, as well as outrageous proposals like the following: *Klkj, lsldffoihs, 3093, lkflsjdsf!*

I'm afraid that what you've just read, and by that we refer to: *Klkj, lsldffoihs, 3093, lkflsjdsf!* was another harmless joke (*déjà vu*).

Now, let's immerse ourselves in what probably ought to be considered *the* most polemic proposal.

An over-excited Priest and famous Professor in Physics and Biology (we refuse to affect his career, hence, we won't disclose his name unless a worthy sum is forwarded to the editor of this masterpiece), at a conference in Harvard, during the presentation of his last colossal work about beauty, perception, dialectics and aesthetics entitled *I Love How the Consecrated Host Dissolves in my Mouth Like an M&M*, proposed:

What if we place some naked nuns on the altar, as they play their dirty hellish lustful games during the Sunday mass, and the officiating priest, dressed in an angelic uniform, milks them *in situ*? If you don't fancy that, we could pretend the priest is the milked Pinocchio who burns himself up after a passionate display of lavish self-love and makes a triumphal reappearance disguised as the Fairy.

A reckless idea that would find a probable insurmountable difficulty: that of finding pregnant or lactating nuns; or allowing, for instance, cows, sheep, whales or any other lactating mammal to be ordained as divine workers.

The Boston Police had to break in and detain this lunatic old man (whose name we still refuse to reveal, unless... you know), who refused to end his conference; great doses of Valium did the trick, disguised as M&Ms.

Further investigations proved useful when some dangerous bonds were uncovered for the sake of the Catholic Church and Human Kind as well. He – and only because a fair amount of dollars has reached the editor's hand, we are allowed to reveal his first name – Professor of Physics, Biology, and Father Piotr, was a business partner with Geppetto[60] (a.k.a. *Dio* or God), a Sicilian tailor with links inside the '*Ndrangeta*.

He, the Father Piotr, could also have been involved (along with several employees of the Saint Chichastarmic Cathedral) in the trafficking of wooden dolls.[61]

The Opus Dei – alongside the United Federation of Sects and Cults – on the other hand (the left one please) energetically repudiated the famous but still secret Abu Kasem's *Opus Magnum*, required the mysterious author's international capture, claimed that they would have placed the author on their oppressive person list if they had one,

---

60 See: Final Debate
61 See: Origins

and also emphatically denied that they were a vicious porn-adept sect or that they had anything to do with child exploitation and harassment, or with any other unlawful sexual practice outside the holy sacrament of marriage. Lastly, they strongly denied having links with Pinocchio, André Bobassi or Will and the Pear Shakes.[62]

The funny thing is that there were no accusations whatsoever about those matters above mentioned.

The Professor's complete name is Piotr Illych Molineronke.

This chronicle is about to reach its end, and the clouds are about to cry.

---

62 See: Consufion

Cultural Beliefs

Every culture, every society, has its own corpus of beliefs and superstitions: djinns, aluxes, gnomes, leprechauns, and so forth.

Western society suffers from both: belief in freedom to choose and its subsequent superstition, called democracy.

The first, suggests that there is something more.

The second, that there is something less.

Delusional Idealism

To believe that by forbidding, the forbidden vanishes.

The Intention

That dream you are after may become a nightmare
Such things exist not in wakefulness;
Only problems to be solved and realities to be accepted
The intention is the dream of the awake.

Wanting and Desiring

Wanting without desiring is a mark of detachment.

Desiring without even wanting is a mark of conditioning.

The key is attachment.

Because that's what desire is:

Attachment to that which is wanted.

Desire is a veil that separates you from the now.

Adam, Eve and the Fruit

As we enjoy the enormous privilege of smelling and also of being able to read by thus offering our very eyes such a marvellous literary feast – and yes we are referring to the original copy of our admired Abu Kasem's anthological masterwork – we feel some sort of urge to share with you, beloved readers (though we are uncertain how many of you there are... if there are indeed any), some pages from this infinite best-seller, which by the way has nothing to do with any privileged member of the Peter Sellers family, entitled *Opus Magnum*.

Bonding ourselves with chance, we thus open the masterpiece as we empty ourselves of expectancy, and with a feather-light ego we read:

> The simple but yet puzzling matter of the apple as the fundamental symbol of human disobedience which in turn gave way to evil and its pairing off with that lavish and tempting serpent, could be of such unexpected depth that we are obliged to inform those readers who are in this very moment ingesting these lines, to

stop right away if your swimming abilities are not at least proficient or if you are without the proper accompaniment.[63]

Such a depth, that goes far beyond the common imagination, might even hide within it samples of the ugliest human vileness, as well as the most evil[64] manipulations ever witnessed by men, or women, or puppets,[65] or blind folks, or shamans, or cooks, or woodpeckers, or sweaty pianists, or Abbots, or Costellos.

I'm afraid that I might have been unclear in my description of how grave the matter is to us all and the type of ulterior impact it had on human history. In fact, this subject is so serious that no man, or woman, or puppet, or *ad libitum ad imaginatus* could have been capable of performing such evil

---

63 Such a statement was a personal recommendation of Abu Kasem's barrister, due to several unwanted watery accidents during the first editions of this chronic; though we are indeed happy to share that, to this day, no fatal drowning victims are accounted for. Common sense indicates that proper accompaniment implies someone or something that might aid during the navigation of such deep waters, which of course, have nothing to do with Roger or with Muddy.

64 On occasions we can find within the realms of the *Opus Magnum* a recurrence of certain overstatements in some of the probable author's personal views on things (Ed.). You will notice that a bit further down, dear reader, you shall be able to find another example of this. It seems that the editor had some trouble in choosing one of the many options that the author left in the air (subcontracted Ed.).

• Commentary on the previous note: Seems to us that someone less than proficient in English translation could have worked on this copy (TN.).

65 See: Opprobrium

acts, except for some characters which we are to depict in the following lines, whose existence I can regrettably inform you of.

Thus, a stroke of our wordy brush will enlighten the readers about these beasts that once trod on this earth; but I do hope that it is already clear enough that those horrendous acts and stratagems could not have been created and perpetrated by just an ordinary man, or woman...[66]

During my research undertaken by myself,[67] in order to finally compile this enlightening book, I came across contradicting versions, which varied according to who the collector, or manipulator, was.

The Benedictine monk baptized as Rafael de la Turba, but who everybody in his hometown referred to simply as 'stupid little man', born exactly eight hundred years ago[68] in what now

---

66 Ed. – On occasions, the probable translator and not the writer himself resorts to an over-clarification of a given subject. We are not sure if it's a memory problem or something related to insecurities forged during his early ages. (Of course, this is not a mere repetition of the joke expressed in both *previous footnotes*, which in this case, because it's a plural form, ought to be *feetnotes*.)

67 You must pardon the language inaccuracies, but we intend to preserve the texts in their original form.

68 We believe that there's a certain relationship between the date on which the author worked on the referred chapter and the birth of our champion. That singular moment of genius still can't be placed in time; hence, we can't possibly know when the aforementioned was born (de la Turba). *Geniality is a never-ending thread that embraces both beginning and end*, Radamés Washington "π" Funes Da Silva, S*elected Sitted Poems.*

is called Torrejón de Ardoz, near the actual city of Madrid, explains to us that:

"The inclusion of the apple as the prohibited fruit leads us to one name, that of San José de las Termas, third copyist of the manuscript that inspires these very same lines, which was inherited by Andrés, who used to be Simon Peter's second maternal cousin, and which was obtained through an obscure riña de gallos *that for reasons which are far from logical accepted the palimpsest as a betting pledge, to finally end, somewhere in this* cojonudo *universe, over the triumphant and manipulative hands of the victor* gallo,[69] *that is to say, San José's."*

According to Rafael's sole and modest contribution to the ever-expanding realm of literature through his *Memorias de un gran masturbador*, San José could have very well suffered an irreparable hence terrible loss during a grey and stormy day, precisely in the course of the fourth day of the month of April, throughout the 126th year in the Era of our Lord Jesus Christ.[70]

We are, of course, referring to that loss which is the greatest of them all for an innocent child;

---

69 We opt to include the original word in order to avoid stating: the victor's cock.

70 About meteorological circumstances and forgotten historical events, do not hesitate to consult the revolutionary approach to the subject by the Flemish embalmer, Jaan van der Meerkewarden in his *L'Histoire de l'Histoire Météorologique*.

the decease of his creators (or should we better call them simply copyists, given that the only God is the source of all creation?). That is, of course, the death of both his parents, a.k.a. *mamá y papá*; Edith and Simón.

How could this have occurred?

Given the bizarre circumstances in which such a dreadful event took place, the real reasons are hard to uncover; but as all ways lead to Rome, all clues lead to apples.

It is quite certain that in those days, given the lack of proper instruments and tools, it was almost (or should we say indeed?) impossible to deduce how the terrible accident happened. The traumatized boy, a six-year-old San José, found his copyists (or shall we indeed call them creators, given that everything that is created is indeed a *creatio ex Deus*, they being mere instruments of the Divine Grace?), or better said parents, half-naked, half-dressed but completely lifeless, under the triumphant apple tree. That was the wretched scene that our little hero had tried (vainly) to comprehend. The rest are mere theories aimed at finding a feasible explanation destined to content those logical minds which are satiated by mere probabilities.

Taking into account all the possible factors that could have had a certain influence, be those big, small or thunderous, I cannot escape the theory that such elements as astrological coordinates, weather conditions, and other questions that I shall reserve to myself, conjure within my logical mind. Everything indicates that the passing was due to the impact of a pair of those red little and severe fruits also known as *malus pumila*;[71] a fall that found its end on both *mamá*'s and *papá*'s heads, as they were both intimately bonded under the shade offered by the treacherous apple tree,[72] recreating that treasured moment in which she got pregnant for the first time in her life (and, alas, last), thus becoming San José's vessel.

For those unaccustomed to such an erudite use of the language, we simply state that they were copulating, or fornicating if you prefer, under this tree that ended up losing – though it's not possible to judge the tree's intention, according to common sense, but others think in

---

71 Santino Marcosse, an Italian linguist and expert in forgotten Latinisms, draws a remarkable comparison between the technical word for the apple of paradise, *malus pumila*, and the Latin word *malum* or *malus*, that expresses *wrongness, wrongdoing, something that should be performed in another way*. At the same time, he points out that the apple had appeared *after* the genesis, hence *before* the story that bonds us together, in Homer's fifth book of the *Iliad*, when Eris, the Greek goddess of chaos and discord, exposed the vanity of Hera, Athena and Aphrodite during the feast after the celebration of the wedding between Peleus and Thetis. Perhaps, its most glorious appearance occurs in *Das Rheingold*.

72 Some say that it could not have happened under the shade, since it was a rainy day. One of those voices is that of Marcus Grünnewald, author of *Wege der Metheorologischen Natur*.

a different fashion[73] – a couple of apples that happened to land on the lovers' heads (superior in the case of his father), inducing in them an everlasting slumber, or death if you dislike metaphors.

Bad (or good) fortune intervened, helping the first apple to harshly hit Simón's (*papá*) crest, causing as a result the instant loss of his erection. But fatally for both, he did not only lose it due to the distraction created by the falling fruit (not referring to his banana, but to the descending apple), he also allowed his somehow weak Taoistic control to vanish, which logically implied that he could no longer hold his sticky milky essence inside – where it belongs unless the lover decides that the *ripe* moment is nigh[74] – thus tarnishing his wife's dress as he nervously attempted to remove his member from her interior in order

---

73 Biologist and weightlifter Sir John Pao has expressed recently in a very famous Sunday magazine, which is part of the biggest newspaper in the world, that *certain experiments are being carried out in order to prove not only that trees are sensitive, but they can develop some kind of what could be seen as human feelings, such as jealousy, anger, loneliness and fondness of football. This is why I think that the nowadays discussed theme of the apple as the forbidden fruit and the unfortunate accident that San José's parents suffered, was not an accident by force of chance at all, but the price his mother had to pay after flirting and blatantly seducing a married apple tree.*

74 See: Similarities

to (hopelessly) avoid another Shakespearean moment.[75]

This outer garment had been a precious gift made by the right hand of the King – and hairdresser in his spare time – as a payment for certain obscure favours she had provided; some still think that such favours were indeed of a sexual nature, whereas others think that she only used to bring him fresh ale every Sunday morning.

This unfortunate accident – and by *this* we are not referring to the fall of the apple, nor to the banana-crumble or the *coitus interruptus* but to the stained dress – inspired Edith's (*mamá*) uncontrollable anger, expressed by her left hand, precisely the one that slapped Simón on his left cheek[76] with hateful dexterity and strength, thus instantly depriving him of the miracle of life.[77]

---

75 See: Consufion
76 This subject is one which inspires great controversy, given the fact that it's hard to understand how she managed to slap her husband's left cheek using her opposite (left) hand. The use of an inverted technique (like the old-school tennis backhand shot, impacting with the palm or its upper side) or a fake arm should not be discounted; or perhaps, a piece of wood that merely **resembled** a human arm.
77 A fervent right-wing leader of the Republican Party of New Gondwanaland expresses the view in his weekly column featured in his 6-year-old son's school bulletin, that *if read in an allegorical fashion, we can learn from history and recognize that the secret message of this soon to be biblical story is that left-wing politicians and probably sportsmen of any kind as well will suddenly appear and kill you.* Signed by Rupta Abescassis.

History scholars have, since then, passionately debated – and some even went to extreme duellistic stages – about the primordial reason that caused and inspired the mortal blow. Some think that the fundamental cause of such rage was the supposed uncontrolled semen expulsion caused by a petty fruity distraction, which was helped by Simón's lack of perineum strength; a fact (the uncontrolled ejaculation) that was fervently disowned during such times and apparently had been a frequently rehashed topic during the couple's therapy sessions they had been enduring for months at that stage.

Others, that the ruining stain that transformed the gorgeous dress into an *ad aeternum* piece of crap was the violence's seed.[78]

A ridiculous number of disregarded communist scholars firmly believe that this article is worthless and should not be read.

Nevertheless, the vast majority of historians, theologians and scholars simply concur with the idea that she was a crazy bitch.[79]

According to MIT physics, the left hand hit/ blow/collision, in order to prove deadly for such a fit and healthy man as Son José's father – he was the strongest man of the hamlet for thirty-four

---

78 For more details about these reactions, please consult *History of an Unexpected Visit*, chapter entitled '*The effect of noises and sudden outbursts*' by René Guennwsa, 1943.

79 Plutarco said, *dementiae merda est.*

consecutive years – must have been of such a force that, 0.00005786 seconds after the impact, an expansive wave of 87.6 Hz must have occurred, thus inducing the fall of the second deadly apple on her head.

That's how the objective chronicles of San José de las Termas' late parents end.

Now, forcing ourselves into more adventurous, wondrous, monstrous, tuberous and rugged paths, we can naturally infer that the previous tragedy could have become, in Aristotle's words, ...

Of course, Aristotle is dead, reason why we left those .... as a symbol of silence. But being much more precise and faithful to the written expression, we shall rephrase the last paragraph in order to carry on peacefully.

Now, forcing ourselves into more adventurous, wondrous, monstrous, tuberous and rugged paths, we can infer naturally that the previous tragedy could have become, and expressing it as Aristotle would have written it or said it if he were still alive (provided that we could make sense of what his toothless mouth or his shaky handwriting could have been expressing at this very moment), the primordial engine that fuelled our back-then-innocent-hero but today-surely-ashes-underground San José and his rascally and impious modifications of the holy Scriptures, placing the hated apple at the centre of ignominy as the forbidden fruit, hence becoming the origin of the posterior disequilibrium experienced throughout human history.

He left these words on the pages of his personal diary:

The fall of the apple is the fall of human kind; the banished species from paradise. I can't blame the one and only almighty God for this, but I will make the treacherous apple pay for my everlasting pain and persistent virginity.

It might be useful to recall that the actual original Genesis – we are not referring to the Progressive Rock British band, though its original formation with Peter Gabriel on vocals/flute is regarded as the best in their history – was lost around 4,760 BC, in a yet-to-be-determined area along the sands of the Negev desert; according to a dream experienced and then retold by the Abbot of the Negrotti Cathedral Johannus Swederborg, the primal word uttered to mention the forbidden fruit could have sounded approximately like *Alkooon gjhaaaadiaf jasidaeh.*[80]

---

80 An experimental form of phonetics during the early stages of the Aramaic language is being shared here thanks to the generosity of the National Museum. If you wish to utter the quoted words, follow these instructions:
- Take a shower
- Then, take your soaking wet clothes off, and hang them in order to be sun dried
- If there is no sun, wait. This step cannot be avoided
- Once the garments are being caressed by the sun, get dressed using only white clothes and sandals made of cork
- Spit on your right foot
- Make your Labrador dog lick the spit
- If you happen to not have a dog, get one, and respect the breed. It must be a Labrador
- If you can't get a dog because you are afraid of them, go to therapy

(continued)

Sir Alan Robbins, lecturer in dead, forgotten and prohibited languages, forged an acceptable translation of such a term, after forty years of hard work that appeared to be endless; his humble approximation is:

Exquisite fruit that after the first bite expels an amazing scent, and its flavour will make your legs succumb; but then it shall become a potent aphrodisiac and you will have intercourse with your lady wife or any other biped who happens to be in your vicinity.

We trust that these events, dear reader, under the infallible guidance of the Supreme Being who leaves nothing to chance, will open a vast panorama of a wild rainbow of possibilities to be enjoyed as well as interpreted.[81]

Now that chance appears to have a tiny part of the Lord's favour, we choose one of those rational extravaganzas.

- If you don't believe in Freudian methods, choose an alternative approach of your liking i.e. California Flowers
- Once the spit is licked, go to the kitchen and get a red apple
- If you happen to keep your apples in another room that is not the kitchen, proceed to take the red fruit to the kitchen, leave the room and re-enter it in order to get the apple
- Bite the apple, and without chewing, take a sip of water
- With both water and the first apple bite in your mouth, say these words: "Jesus is an Ant, and I am his Witness." That is how early Aramaic sounded.

81 It is fair to say that if the Lord is the sole source of all qualities and merits, it shan't be possible that He leaves nothing to chance. His generosity is such, that even chance, randomness, surely enjoys a portion of His divine giving spirit (Ed.).

Pierre Montenaux de Perpignan, a renowned Franciscan monk, tells us in his *Historiae Universalis Frutae* that:

The inclusion of the apple, both in the Genesis and the annals of literature, is an idea forged by Guillaume D'Avignonaisse Tellousian, historically referred to as William Tell. Well known was his love for bow and arrow, and his fondness for apples. According to some now missing personal letters, William had a suspicious and more-than-friendly relationship with the Cardinal in charge of the Rhin region, Alfred Maunschitz, who by chance happened to have a huge network of agents working within the Vatican; this not only helped him to gain valuable information about the intimacies of several high members of the Holy State, but to amass a huge fortune as well: Agel, Herbalife and Amway were some of the brands he used to sell in that tricky and capitalist pyramidal marketing scheme... or shall we say scam?

Whether or not it is indeed not ethical to determine the nature of their friendship, we must present the two theories that carry this story's gossipy weight.

The first one indicates that after enjoying luscious and dairy sexual favours, Herr Maunschitz really found pleasure in watching Mr Tell who, after the performance of such devilish and punishable affairs, used to adopt bizarre poses; the couple's favourite was the one in which the archer held an apple between his teeth, pretending to be a human *canard à l'orange*, or correctly written *canard à la pomme*.[82]

The fourth one (being in reality the theory number two, but I'm too superstitious to use the words that describe those places between the first and the fourth) indicates that Guillaume D'Avignonaisse Tellousian, our famous William Tell, suffered a terrible loss due to a missed *Apfelschuss*. In fact, not only one but seven severe mistakes that ended his seven masculine children's' joyful lives. Not being able to recover himself from such a dramatic turn of events, he recurred to his lifelong friend, Herr Maunschitz, in order to pay tribute to his deceased sons; he needed to see the red bloody fruit in the centre of human infamy; the depiction of the lowest treacherous act that could ever be committed by human kind: that of disobeying the Lord and therefore condemning the whole posterity to an unbearable separation from the source. Thus, taking advantage of Herr M's connections – who also in this theoretical history not only had lots of friends in the Vatican but who was not rich nor took advantage of that capitalist

---

82 In this particular case, the apple might have been painted in orange colour. This could explain the origin of the Spanish saying, that inaccurately translated reads like *when oranges are absent, suffice the oranged-apples*. Found in *Origin and History of Spanish Collection of Sayings of Middle Europas*, signed by Carl María von Schmack.

pyramidal scheme – Guillaume D'Avignonaisse Tellousian made sure that the apple was to be placed in that very tree that would end up inhabiting the Parnassus of ignominy, mirroring his own fall into a living son-less Hell.

If I were forced to choose one, that would be theory number two, or the one that goes between the first theory and the absence that exists as a result of adding two more to the first. I can do it; I can break the spell; the arcane fear can be overcome. I choose the second...

Thus ends the *Historiae Universalis Frutae*, with the sudden death of the superstitious and erudite Pierre Montenaux de Perpignan.

In order to help the reader regain balance and common sense, it is indeed worth noting and mentioning that the name of William Tell is quoted in Idries Shah's *The Way of the Sufi*, page 14.

But, returning to our favourite fruity matter, some secret sources within the Holy City in Rome whisper about certain *affaires* involving the late *alma pater* of a most successful computer company whose brand logo is, predictably, a *malus pumila*.

The reason?

Negotiations concerning a new Bible, including a whole re-scripture and modernisation of our Holy Book following the *à la mode* print-on-demand model.

The aim?

To remove the apple from the ignominy's throne, after ages of fraudulent manoeuvres perpetrated by egomaniacal men; to eternally dislodge the round and red fruit from the Adamic disgrace and the posterior link with the human fall, as well as its relationship with God's wrath; to completely devour the apple and leave a simple seed as a trade logo: a seed to be spat into the new paradise to come which will, fruitfully, give birth to a new and pure apple tree.

The substitutional variation?

Instead of having an apple tree as a dominative figure in the famous paradisiacal scene, we would embrace – thanks to the benefits of a *creatio ex nihilo* – a new form of plant whose branches would bear not apples, of course, but a to-be-determined product of the rival firm. If this proves to be hard-to-believe in the soon-to-occur focus group testings, a vast house made of pure windows shall not be discarded as a replacement for the tree. The primordial couple, instead of biting the forbidden fruit could, for instance, have tremendous problems with their brand new laptop, or might be unable to enter their windowed home due to an update complication which keeps them away from paradise.

Clever and agile as usual, the *Alma pater* of the very same company that could be accurately described as the house with a thousand windows, contacted his lifelong friend Pinocchio in order to plan a massive-scale contamination of a certain part of Africa and some *shitty third world Latin countries* (our sources claim that this *Alma pater* uttered such offensive epithets with a furious gesture coronated by the foam coming out of his mouth) using red apples. As part of the same operation, art scouts are trying to find a future star painter, who would be in charge of creating the definitive masterpiece that will win the technological and siliconial war, for once and for all.

The painting's motif?

A candid and pastoral scene: oblivious of their surroundings, Adam and Eve are enjoying a lovely Sunday picnic whilst listening to some demonic music on their personal mp3 players; they are in hell – precisely because they ignore it – feasting on their deceased offspring's flesh.

Radamés Washington "π" Funes Da Silva, using his usual educational and easy-going tone, closes this chapter saying:

> It is very true that the legend of the forbidden fruit has been subjected to endless mutations throughout time, though the same could be argued about any other probable myth. In some isolated cloisters, where the usual contact with women of low esteem was almost impossible, and the acquaintance with women of high esteem was definitely worse than impossible, a tropical banana was introduced as the forbidden fruit in the medieval version of the Genesis, for obvious, posterior, dark, sometimes hairy, predictable reasons.
>
> A vast number of complicated variations of the original tale that have been recently discovered find their origin in those lightless times; for instance, through changing the popular *and Eve bit the fruit* for the more reprehensible *and Eve*

shoved the fruit – banana – down[83] *a certain orifice not meant for that particular purpose.* For those distracted readers, the previous sentence refers to the bottom hole. The same applies to Adam, of course.[84]

Under this light, the Genesis becomes probably the first sexual investigation of our era, describing not only some unorthodox and rare erotic endeavours, but inspiring different usages and perhaps the vibrating inventions of elements that today are commonly used in every household across the globe.

Some lines after, the generous and enlightening Radamés Washington "π" Funes Da Silva shares some interesting facts:

During the big drought in Côte d'Ivoire that took place in the beginnings of the twentieth century, Colonel Tito Drogba took advantage

---

83 The debate is still very much alive as to whether the word should be *down* or *up*. Unless Eve had advanced yogic (although at the time yoga had not been yet created, so if we accept this surmise as possible we shall regard her as the creator of the discipline of Yoga) abilities in order to do a *Sirsasana* (please be it noted how it rhymes with banana) and the help of Adam, it is very much clear that the word used should have been *up*.

84 If that would have been correct, the Wrath of God should be bartered into the Laugh of God, by the sight of such an infantile and harmless deed. Joseph Guiseppini thus writes in his *Three Hundred Ways to Eat a Piece of Fruit.*

of likely literary inventions in order to palliate the lack of coconuts. As a consequence, the palm tree became the forbidden-fruit bearer in an Eden placed within the African continent.

In the Old World, during the crazy cow epidemic, the EU parliament and its committee of sages pondered the possibility of removing the apple and introducing a hanging cow in the Holy Scriptures. The most prestigious inhabitants of the cultural world were consulted in order to create the definitive paragraph that would make the animalesque variation both feasible and effective. The last presented draft contained the following sentence:

"... *and Eve grabbed the cow with utmost gentleness, detaching her from its branch, as Adam was preparing a nice fire using his own faeces and Pinocchio as combustible fuel. She failed to restrain her voracious appetite and tried to remove a portion of the ill-fated animal with her bare teeth; but tough as the beef was, she lost a couple of her incisors. Adam, with tender love, showed her the way to the fulfilment of the flesh, macerating the about-to-be-eaten cow with spices and sauces till the perfect cooking texture was achieved. Finally, both enjoyed a fucking great barbecue.*"

The definitive draft was lastly revised by the Cardinal Jacinto González Gómez Pérez, member of the diocese of Guijón. It was ultimately discarded because of a simple but fatal detail: mankind had not yet discovered fire and, as a natural consequence of that lacking of know-how, the art of cooking; and most importantly, in those crazy cow times it was not at all sensible to eat raw cow meat.

If the truth were to be told, this subject would carry on *ad libitum*, *ad aeternum*, *ad imaginatus*. I resign myself to keep writing (and exploring) its infinite permutations inside this marvellous toilet of mine; this court-room; this hollowed and illuminated watery throne that accepts me fully, reigning over a lost street in Nueva Palmira.

Thus closes his chapter XXI, perhaps endless, the great Radamés Washington "π" Funes Da Silva.

Mysteries Unveiled

Taking advantage of the great privilege that implies a conscious scrutiny of the endless pages from our beloved *Opus Magnum*, we quote some curious observations about books that were previously published, and also from those drafts that were judged as unworthy of the thickness of the ink; from books that are going to be published in a probable near future, and of those *oeuvres* judged undeserving of the marketing charades that are typical of the oligarchical publishing houses; also we shall not forget those books that are not to be published in the unforeseeable future: belonging to all those probabilities or certainties are some of these observations, both worthy and unworthy of your precious time, dear reader.

The personal views of the anthropologist, filmmaker, poet, *regisseur*, asthmatic and scholar of La Fontaine and Aesop's fables, Jean Marie Eugueniçe Ramboulleou, are contained within the pages of her last work – and only – entitled *Fables, Croissants and Canard à l'Orange.*

The third chapter which summons us here is entirely dedicated to the supposed existence of the super-duper famous Prince Charming, better known by Latin underdeveloped and third world cultures as *El Príncipe Azul* or *Principe Azzurro*. That is, through *verbatim* translation, the Blue Prince.[85]

His following analysis is perfectly justified given his Italian and Spanish ancestry; the reader might realize swiftly that his name is merely an artistic mask to cover his real original denomination: Juan María Eugencia Cazzalli del Hortelano. He wrote:

The *Principe Azzurro* was a real man, and not a gigantic Smurf. I strongly defy those peyotistic theories that present our lovely and divine member of the royalty of fables as an over-developed little fungus creature. His nobility title was bestowed upon him not only because he inherited it, but also due to his impressive yet humble presence; and also thanks to a subtle garmental detail: the cape that, caressing his neck, covered his delicate and slender figure, carved and shaped through endless hours of yoga, Pilates and kettlebell swings; nevertheless, he wore it far too tightly around his swanlike neck, hence the blue reference.

---

85 Maybe this is a great occasion to comment about the possibility that the *Principe Azzurro* is simply a colloidal silver addict, whose effects – among others – are the blueification of the human skin, as well as the infamous storyteller's syndrome, which makes the sufferer fall into a constant delusion: the sense that he is constantly living in a fairy tale. We shall accept that the Prince could as well be really a Smurf in favour of the monarchic dialectics which are nowadays in vogue.

Each morning, when he left the family home, his over-protective Italian-style mother would almost strangle him – adjusting the cape around his neck – whilst complaining about how he never took proper care of himself, that the weather was too cold for his fragile health, and that if something happened to him she would instantly die, not before slaying the whole town.

This feminine co-creator was known by all in her hometown as *porca putana*, yet her family called her by her Christian name: Silvia D'Ancoli, a suffering woman whose life was one of abandonment. She was barely three years old when her father, a ruthless merchant from Vercelli, left Silvita and *mamma* Carla in utter pennilessdom; without uttering a single word, he sneaked out into the twentieth night of the ninth month of that very same year, never to return.

Her life passed through those greenish eyes in a grey and unnoticed manner, until an encounter that precisely occurred as she was suffering her first flourishing bleed promised to be, perhaps, a light after the nine-year-long fatherless tunnel. Suddenly, life seemed to be great; he was tall, handsome, blessed with rugged looks and a perfect Greek profile; there was even something familiar about such a breathtaking presence. He was known by everyone as Andoni. The connection between them was passionate and instantaneous. The very same butcher shop

that became an involuntary witness of this first
encounter was also the love nest that, through
the stench of its cow juices and the mystical scent
of sausages, inspired the three-month couple
to bond forever in the act of physical love. The
result of that union was a baby who, due to a
minor problem with the umbilical cord, almost
died at birth. His colour was anguishing; colour
that in the end proved to be a premonition for
what was to become his own destiny: he was
named Azzurro, which means 'blue' in English.

Three years after that birth, which of course
took place at the very same butcher shop that
had been forced to witness the three most special
moments in their lives, the Norns of fate kept
weaving their inescapable web; life had other
plans: it defecated and vomited once again in
povera Silvia's face when a wordless Andoni, her
true and only love, snuck into the night, thus
leaving her and the *piccolo* Azzurro in the usual
anguished abandonment, never to return.

Of course, these are not simply theories of
mine, but the result of a huge number of hours
of investigations and study, which led and
eventually helped me to find a secret dossier
strategically placed under a simple and beautiful
monument honouring Madame Curie's work,
adorning a humble café in the outskirts of Basra.

In that document I found lots of microbes,
mites, an autographed picture of the great
Enrico Caruso, a single red hair that apparently

belonged to the not-so-great David Caruso, and bits of iron dust that might have once belonged to Daniel Larusso's bike. Apart from these curious findings, I could read some observations made by Jools Vixsundermanft, a well-known professor of the University of Le Havre and the Collegium Rotterdamer, written on the margins of the unnamed Basra Dossier:

2 spoons of salt, 35 grams of sugar, 50 little Smurfs…

It is easy to see that those notes have nothing to do with the matter that gathers us around my book. The interesting ones express that:

"The real name of our debated monarch, the mythical *Principe Azzurro*, is (because he shall be eternal) Giuseppe Carlo Rigoberto del Paccino, and indeed what an Apollonian shaveling he was! Sorry! He *was*, *is* and *will be*, given his eternal quality. He was, is, and will be a man blessed by the gods; even from his tender age he heard the ovine vocational whisper through which he knew that sheep were supposed to be his life and true passion.

"Giuseppino wasted no time in worldly tasks: he submerged himself at once into a dedicated practice that was meant to hone his skills as a *pastorello*; and bonded with a digestive system that abhorred the abundant Piamontese rice, he swiftly set out in the search of true heights where his only true and woolly friends would be expecting him in order to begin to settle his ovine fate.

"He found everything amongst those rocky heights of Monte Barone, which by force of chance or gentleness of fate were suitably close to his hometown of Vercelli.

"Coming back to his woolly love: such was the natural inclination of affection that Giuseppino felt towards his shepherding vocation and his ovine friends, that he used to improvise sung stanzas about how there could be no damsel capable of equalling the sheltering interior of his beloved sheep; here we shall see a key element which perhaps might explain some of his exceptional exploits: such woolly predilection might shelter the reason why I do believe that our blueish shepherd was able to perform so many unselfish acts throughout the history of fairy tales with such astonishing detachment. I'm sure that the smell and warmth of his beloved sheep inspired him to kiss and rescue all those wretched blonde female characters, with the latent and innermost intention of helping them discover and enjoy, in peace and harmony, the taste, warmth and love that his little woolly sheep exuded and offered to him, on the rocky heights of Monte Barone.

"His false name finds its origin in our hero's out-of-control consumption and abuse (both

culinary and physical) of Blue Cheese, or
Gorgonzola. Narratives of his time[86] speculate
about his cheesy diet regime; it is widely
believed in the northern part of Italy, where
his home town was, that the *Principe* – that
is, Giuseppe Carlo Rigoberto del Paccino –
ingested between seven hundred eighty-six and
eight hundred seventy-four kilos of Roquefort
per day, depending on his body temperature and
the circumstantial accompaniment with whom
he enjoyed and shared the dairy delicacy. His
feast usually began at 7.31 am, at the precise
moment his family cock offered his first chant,
though this did not always occur in the same
fashion; sometimes our blueish Giuseppino
was awakened by the unconscious yet hard
singing of his own cock; something which
naturally forced him out of bed in search of the
cleansing waters, both to wash himself and the
stained sheets. If this occurred during a night
without humidity, his parents, or better said,
mamma Silvia and the occasional boyfriend,
would as well suffer the consequences of
the cocky-dreamy-milky-sticky-chant: an
occurrence perhaps favoured by the dry and
unswelled cracks which overpopulated the
sloppy wooden floor that allowed the milky
sticky waterfall's leakage to find its descending

---

86   It is still ignored which time that is (Ed.).

sprouting way from our Giuseppino's bed, who used to wake up not only inundated by pleasure, but also accompanied by the inferior shouts coming from the maternal chambers; a constant duet, yet not always expressing the awaited repugnance in unison. It is my honest opinion that the recurrence of his sticky milky watery dreams was due to the irresistible charm of those gorgeous sheep shepherded by him – sorry again! That he shepherded, shepherds and will do so, given that Giuseppe is, was and will always be eternal.

"His cheese consumption ended at midnight, yet not through force of will or gustatory predilections, but due to a blockage of the airways: this usually became evident when some undigested inches of the blue delicacy made their appearance out of his left nostril."[87]

Following Jools Vixsundermanft's marginal remarks, I was not able to stop reading. After some scarce minutes, and written in black dense ink on the very reverse of the page on which I had found the previous notes, I read:

---

87 Town-famous was his chronic constipation. In fact, still today in his village one can hear about his lavatory myth: it is believed that after discovering the blue delicacy, he was not able to ever expel his internal waste again. *Gone with the Cheese*, John Pilergherman (1978).

"Of course, these former speculations make the most sense! Thanks dear Jools for enlightening me in what so far for me has been the biggest mystery in human history: why was Silvia D'Ancoli perpetually suffering from a coupleless state, without being able to re-establish herself through another bond of love thus healing her emotional soul, if she indeed was an astonishingly beautiful *mamma* with breasts that could feed the entire town and also produce the vast amounts of cheese required by her only child, Giuseppe Carlo Rigoberto del Paccino?

"That very account of Giuseppe's wet dreams offers the solution to a problem that has pushed me to an almost inevitable suicide. She (*la mamma*) always ended up dating soulless men who took advantage of the free watery-milky-sticky-fall that appeared *ex nihilo* in Silvia's bedroom during those dry mornings. I do firmly believe that this is why she could never establish a proper and steady relationship with any real and worthy man of noble and altruistic soul; some of them were completely homosexual and only loved her just out of the watery-milky-fall interest they had, whereas others were strictly heterosexual yet unable to resist the chance of being fed in the mouth with such a mysterious nourishment that appeared to come from the heavens, as if it were a divine *manna*.

"Is it fair to imagine that most of her meaningless affairs were with Jewish men, eager and desperate to seek for the divine sign of Yahweh in the watery-milky-sticky-fall? Maybe we shall see in the circumcision suffered by those self-interested Hebrews, the metaphor of a lacking part, of the absent love away from *mamma's* bed, which brimming of dairy interest thus symbolizes the absence of a true connection between Silvia D'Ancoli and men in general?

"I do also assume, through a severe exercise of sincerity, that if I have had the chance to sleep in that sticky bed, I surely could have not refrained myself from taking a loaf of bread at night to then hide it under the pillow; afterwards, when the bread shall be warm as a consequence of several hours under my head and bearing the right dose of my saline sweat in conjunction with the natural grease found in my hair, I would probably enjoy the sticky-milky-watery-fall with my toasted banquet and perhaps some slices of *prosciutto*; why not also have my coffee with a bit of fresh and lukewarm milk as well? Who is such a hypocrite that would not only censor but despise and condemn the behaviour of those interested lovers? O cruel destiny which never granted Silvia a man suffering from lactose intolerance!"

I wish I could share the name of the author of those powerful insights, but apparently he had run out of ink; though it seems that he did try to continue to write with an unidentified milky-sticky substance, which I cannot distinguish through taste nor sight.

That very same ink (or milky-sticky substance) which found its primal cause in those wondrous inspirations which came in endless heavenly currents to the now former president of the Ottoman Society of Suicidal Writers, Abdul Malik al Mazur, shakes our intellectual drowsiness by presenting his very personal conclusions:

"...On the other hand,[88] in order to end this debate about why the Prince is blue, some sources within the inner circle of trust of Sleeping Beauty – whose real name is Marigold Ferregnatti – could have confessed that, in reality, the Prince was indeed an overgrown Smurf.[89] Others believe that he was in fact Smurfette, after the justice department of Merton Council, located in the southwest part of the city of London, ruled in favour of her/his own appeal for a free-of-charge gender exchange.

---

88 Not possible to state which hand that is (Ed.).
89 Previously foreseen in the footnote number (1) of this same narrative. *Chapeau* dear editor!

"What seems to be a fact agreed by all is that which is already a part of the cultural inheritance of humanity: Smurfette was indeed a creation of Gargamel, perpetrated with the sole intention to alter – by using her – the natural balance found within the Smurf's habitat; and you, dear reader, should know by now that she was a gorgeous brunette who became blonde after a frenetic night in which Papa Smurf worked tirelessly in order to transform her into a real Smurf, cleansed from the Gargamelian seal.

"After she becomes a *real* member of the smurfy family, we see that something has changed for good: her hair colour; she is now a blonde.[90] Yet, what still seems to be a matter of great discordance is that apparently – due to some side effects of Papa Smurf's magic tricks, who moved by a certain anxiety to dispossess her from the Gargamelian seal could have made some indolent mistakes – Smurfette got in touch, albeit in an unsuspected way, with her masculine side; this haunted her for days, for weeks, for months. A shadow that eventually inspired her to write an enormous amount of letters to a distant cousin who used to live near

---

90 The overtones of Aryan supremacy are brutal and explicit: the real Smurfette is blonde, whereas the former false one was brunette. The natural question arises without the help of any pharmaceutical aid: Could Papa Smurf have been Hitler? Or at least any of his acolytes? (Ed.)

the Wimbledon Common; it was thanks to one of these lovely epistolary interchanges that Smurfette got to know that something could be done in order to remedy her inner ailment, this brawl with her double *natura*; the rest is history. Through the force of anaesthetics, hormones, supplements and others, full of hope she embraced her masculine side to, once and for all, become the real and only *Principe Azzurro*. Now, I'll dash because all this Smurfette writing has turned me on; I need some Roquefort now!"

These same theories are the examples of what helped Abdul Malik al Mazur reach the end of his scholastic career. A short time after the previous paragraph was published, he was found with a mushroom stuck to his virile member, shouting *Can you feel it, Smurfette?*

Banished from all intellectual circles, he died alone, drowned in the green hellish depths of the Madre de Dios jungle, in Peru. Some weeks before his earthly disappearance, he was last seen in Iquitos, gathering information about clues that, according to what he believed, could have definitely taken him to the ultimate discovery of the real Papa Smurf. All he was carrying was a copy of Tahir Shah's book *Trail of Feathers* and some bucks that he hoped would obtain him some *ayahuasca* sessions.

The now president of the OSSW (whose irrelevant name is unworthy of being mentioned) presents another possibility, given that the *Principe Azzurro*:

Could well have been Papa Smurf, obviously well groomed and without the moustache.

We also have someone else interested in the subject, the eminent Lacanian therapist Ernst Lungwirdt, who confesses:

"I do feel a great aversion towards the *Principe Azzurro*; in the same way that I despise cockroaches, especially when I unwittingly tread on them with my bare feet. All this *surmenage* helped me to realize that the English expression *to feel blue*[91] finds its probable origin in the same existence of the *Principe Azzurro*: he was a man-Smurf, or whatever the reader might like to make of him, whose spirits were always remarkably low.[92] The implications of such a possible assertion are various; that's why I can imply without fear of making a mistake (though I sometimes feel scared, a sentiment that in the end proves its uselessness given that

---

91 Thus, we can easily spot Phil Collins' homage to the Prince himself in his hit song *A Groovy Kind of Love*. Or could it be a tip that leads us toward a huge network of *Principe Azzurro's* worshippers?

92 Further research is being carried out by the AAOHC, which is the American Association of Healthy Cows, aimed at trying *not* to link Gorgonzola consumption and depression. *Nature and Science for the Elite American*, page 2, first column.

I'm never wrong) that the *Principe* lived in a state of chronic depression; thus the origin of the previously quoted expression, which according to Bertrand Russell was used in Welsh taverns in the following fashion: *Hey McCormack, give m'self a Paint, cause me Mary left me, and I feel blue as the Prince.*[93] And moreover, this is the probable reason of the character's name switch: a bout of depression was surely to occur amongst the general population if the fictional character had a name that resembled such a sombre estate of spirits, hence the changeling into a more mild and, let's say, British or Anglo name: *Charming*, much more neutral, harmless, safe."

The subject concerning the Spirit is not being left untouched as I quote Maximal Benedictus Jörg Mustergrumpfel, theologian of the Berlin College of Religions and Sects, who prefigured and wrote a stupendous treaty about myths, fairy-tale characters and dairy products called *Geschichten der Religionen und Mythen*:

"It will all fall into place once we start seeing things on a metaphorical level. Blue is a primary colour of many faculties and purity is precisely one of those. Thanks to my long-time friend

---

93 Bertrand Russell, *About Mathematics and other Wanderings on Fairytale Geometric Patterns*.

Mr James Sittar and his humble generosity (can either of these exist without the other?), I've come to realise the subtle thread that webs beneath that essentiality in the guise of a colour, which in this particular case is *blue*. The word in Arabic for purity is *safwa* (وفـص) in its original form. According to *Lane's Dictionary of Classic Arabic* the primary meaning of the *s-w-f* root is: *It was, or became, clear, limpid, or pure, or free from turbidity, thickness or muddiness, or free from admixture. And, said of the air, or atmosphere: It was, or became, cloudless; free from any particle of cloud. (And it is also said, tropically, of life; and of the mind, or heart; and of love, or affection.)*

"Such are the virtues of that man who is meant to wake up and recognize, through the art of kissing (which might be a prefiguration of all future amatorial experiences), those estranged, fragmented, disoriented and forgotten females soon to become complete women, trapped in the world of appearances, and enslaved by oppression and disguised envy which is a product of the typically masculine misguided competitiveness that has been adopted by them.

"Taking advantage of those illustrative *Lane*'s pages, we scrutinise further meanings of the root *s-w-f* : *He took the clear, or pure, part, or portion of the thing; he took the best, or choice, part, or portion, of it. He regarded him, or acted towards him, with reciprocal purity of mind, or sincerity; or with reciprocal purity, or sincerity, or love, or affection. He made the thing to be his, or he assigned, or appropriated, to him the thing, purely, absolutely, or exclusively.*

"Curiously enough, the Italian word for blue, *azzurro*, might derive originally from the Arab word *azraq* (قرزا), which naturally means blue. *Azraq* doesn't have a wide range of other meanings (it can also mean blindness, and the shining of an arrow-tip or spear), but its letters can be re-arranged to give the word *razzaq* (قازر) in its original Arab writing; this is one of the ninety-nine Divine Names, and means *The Provider, The Providence, The Supplier, The Bestower of Sustenance*, written as *ar-razzaq*. Wahiduddin defines it this way: *The root r-z-q points to the idea of the receiving of anything beneficial, particularly a gift, whereby something is nourished, sustained, or helped to grow physically, mentally or spiritually.*

"The colour blue is merely a symbol for the archetype, the endless form that adopts any possible shape in order to fulfil its task and serve humanity; and in the precise case of our *Principe Azzurro*, the awakening of women (or men or non-binary humans or transgenders in future editions) was his, thus helping them to evolve towards their ultimate goal. Naturally, a literary myth shall replicate itself, but of course not in such an exaggerated fashion; though I have to admit that during my life, I've met remarkable men and women who had certainly gained something that I was never able to find in other mortals: a spark, a shining, a presence, perhaps green, perhaps blue. And of course, also through the force of experience, I have learnt that out here, there are some blueish real workers (though their boss is green), aiming at the full development and evolution of mankind in its entirety. The form is nothing compared to what is contained within."[94]

I was formerly known as Jean Marie Eugueniçe Ramboulleou, whereas my real name is Juan María Eugencia Cazzalli del Hortelano. Now, I've decided to change it to Enriqueta, because that was Sleeping Beauty's real name.

I'm amazed and astonished by all the different types of approaches that I was able

---

94 After the depth of the great Maximal Benedictus Jörg Mustergrumpfel, it's really easy to understand the mechanism that lies within any crystallized religion or esoteric group that lacks the real contact with the source; it has happened with every real contact with Truth throughout history. It was simply a matter of time till the *Principe Azzurro* had its own group of fervent and irrational worshippers. The now world-famous Blue Man Group is the most visible symbol of what could probably be the fastest-growing cult in the world. Other famous adepts include the Mexican pop singer Christian Castro and his radio hit *Azul* and the previously cited Phil Collins and his *A Groovy Kind of Love*. It could be easy to relate every single artistic enterprise with this humble masterpiece, but that's not going to happen. What is indeed a fact, is that every country whose flag has at least a slight touch of some blue, definitely has an operating *Principe Azzurro's* cult or group working in its very bureaucratic guts.

to gather regarding the coloured Prince. I shall leave you, dear reader, to choose the one of your liking. I cannot stop thinking about the grand psychologist Ernst Lungwirdt and his depression theory. If this were to be true, it might be the first time in recorded history where a fictional – not entirely – character has been named after a mental disturbance; or it could be simply the other way around: disturbance mental a after named been has character a where.

NOTE TO THE SECOND EDITION:

While it is indeed impossible to trace the whereabouts of Juan María Eugencia Cazzalli del Hortelano, as it is exceedingly hard to obtain any formal documentation that could assure her mere existence, we are and we shall not be able to erase this account that involves the fairy tale underground.

In fact, even though this very book *is* real, we are still unable to find any of her many quoted texts, not to mention some other mysterious facts which are in utter need of further clarification.

Leaving all that formal nonsense aside, it is nevertheless true that within the realms of traditional oligarchical publishing, whispering echoes can be heard in regard to her probable assassination.

Why?

We don't know. Prince Blue a about all of least, book single a wrote never he or she that and, alive still is he or she that imply necessarily would That. speculated previously had we that direction opposite the in going be could things, fact of matter a As.

---

476 You might have already noticed that there is no reference to this number in the above printed text. Then, carry on reading normally, please?

Limiting Belief

The impossibility of accepting the hypothesis – albeit well documented and real – that speaks of men with true superior knowledge and the ability they have to share it with others as a task of service for humanity, who can be called teachers, is not a sign of the plausibility of such an idea, but of a certain lack of mental flexibility and a certain abundance of limiting beliefs.

People consume books and films of a fantastical nature and, in doing so, they make others wealthy through believing and accepting the *reality* of the fictional characters featured in these works, who are presented as possessing both superior knowledge and the capacity to share it with others.

People ignore the fact that the science fiction genre is being used, among other purposes, in order to make the brain accept certain ideas; had they been featured in a different format, those same ideas would have been immediately discarded as impossible.

People ignore the fact that all fiction has a real base built upon a reality that exceeds the wildest fantasies by far.

People pay to enter a fantasy world which enables them to evade their own realities, thus accepting the feasibility of certain characters and their superpowers; ignoring the fact that, as stated in the first paragraph, those who are the true origin of such fictional characters are offering the possibility for people to face their own true reality, in this world, right now.

The more evident the truth, the more difficult it is to grasp it.

Grimm Brothers

I n the first pages of the chapter numbered after the Romans, that is the MMCI-II of our beloved Master Book, we read the following:

I am sure, dear reader, dear female reader, dear probable reader, dear probable female reader, dear bored reader, dear bored female reader, dear female-probably-concerned-with-household-matters-and-chores reader, dear...[95] that you will remember the intricate personal history of the Grimm brothers, Jacob and Wilhelm; a couple

---

95 Due to questions of sheer pragmatism and space, we interrupt the commencement of the chapter. Given the writer's desire of justice and eagerness put into his work in order not to despise a single soul, the noble and humble Radamés "π" da Silva used 8.456.412 possible combinations of words with the aim of embracing what he believed to be the complete spectrum of probable and potential readers of the *Opus Magnum*, at the precise moment in which he was creating this piece; therefore, no matter what your sexual orientation, or gender, or passion or vocation in life, you are included in one of the probable wordy combinations (Ed.).

of ill-fated siblings who would eventually find their very destiny concealed within their own family name.

So does reminisce the very same biographer and personal sculptor of both genial and sinister *Gebrüder, Graf* – count[96] – von Westphalia, baptised as Edmund von der Wald aus der Rhin, who during his time was already quite famous for his eccentricities[97] and impudence shown towards remarkable and commendable people,[98] as well as for his outstanding skills in *Fussball*,[99]

---

96 I am certain that the noble surname of the German former tennis champion Steffi is worthy of further studies and investigations. The flagrant contradiction between her feminine nature and the clearly masculine surname forces one to think (though I know I'm not yet One and despite the fact that I seldom think yet I am being thought by my commanding self) about the probable effect that anabolic steroids might have had on the athlete's surname; could it be possible that by resorting to performance-enhancing drugs the very nature of one's family name is changed to that of the opposite gender? Is it fair to suspect that before entering the professional tennis circuit, she was known as Steffi Gräffin, which means Countess? *Addendum post-scriptum*: it is indeed lawful to ponder about the value that such a footnote adds to the opus.

97 The Count always tasted his favourite sweets, such as the delicious *Ritter Sport Praline,* on a De Lamerie dish whilst masterfully cutting and placing the delicacy on his mouth with golden cutlery.

98 Among his usual ravings, we find: a middle finger directed at Richard Wagner; a flagrant error during a concert improvised by the Count himself on the very same piano that used to belong to Franz Liszt's hands and heart; and a half eaten *croissant that had been left* in a bad-reputed café in Calais.

99 Sport practised by him until a cruel lesion left him out of the first squad of the SG Wattenscheid 09 team, when he was barely seventeen years old.

synchronised swimming and the ones he displayed whilst playing the typical *rioplatense* card game of *truco* (trick), taught to him by the very same British explorer and famous Sufi, Sir Richard Francis Burton.

Our admired Count Edmund decided to turn his own version of the biography he had previously written about the *Gebrüder* Grimm (which at the time of such creative changeling, had not yet been published) into a novel; a decision he took and vowed to undertake during a warm summer spent on the coast of Amalfi.

In those very days, *Graf* Edmund was recovering from a serious acute bronchitis and a gout attack when, all of a sudden, the stroke of genius occurred: he knew, once and for all, precisely what to do with that boring amount of objective cumulus of names, locations, significant moments in history and dead information that anyone could have recompiled and which tragically are a necessary part of any biography that is worthy of such a name. He sensibly thought that if all the pianists in history merely played what was *not* indicated in the score, all music would sound alike, perhaps identical; but if they were courageous (courage being one of the many faces of sincerity) enough and if they intended to surrender to the Muse of Beauty and Harmony by following the instructions of the music written on the sheet, they would not only find the one truth, but also their own; as a result, that very same piece of music could never sound alike ever again, despite how many times it might be interpreted, both by the same musician (always different every time that the music is being recreated) or any other; whereas those adventurous and courageous real artists would eventually become that which they should have always been: a unity. A perfect recreation through the recreated; the only way to enter the realm of Divine creativity and to step back into the Origin.

Unable to wait a single breath longer, Edmund started to prefigure the way in which to fulfil such a creative, thus colossal task. How to create something worthy of the sweat and the lack of masturbatory hours? How to mix all that dead and meaningless data previously fixed in the form of a biography about a certain couple of brothers, in this case surnamed Grimm? How to turn the Grimm into the Joyful?

The Count understood, once and for all, that if he were to only condemn himself to retell what had already happened in the lives of the immortal *Gebrüder*, it would ultimately be impossible for him to reach the transcendent truth that was waiting to be discovered and then loved; he had to follow his intuitive heart. The sheet or score was the lifespan of both *siblings*, their fate was the music, the performer was the Count, the feather and quill the instrument, and the composer was and is the Mystery Beneath the Veil; the Unnameable; the One Hundredth Name.

Once the epiphany invaded him, he could not leave the Royal Suite until the revolutionary opus was finished. As a sort of *homage* to his beloved Mozart, he wrote the entire piece using music sheets and ink; detail that allowed him to make no corrections, thus breaking free from the fear of failing. The title of his magnanimous opus came in last; it was: *A Marvellous Account of the Exploits of the Beloved, Joyful and Happy Grimm Brothers, a Fableously*[100] *Biographical Novel.* Among many interesting passages and remarks between passionate *fortissimi* and subtle *pianissimi* we can find, according to the *presto* of the reading, certain pearls worthy of the literary Parnassus, such as:

"...I allow myself to quote a cite, or to cite a quote, of the famous duet of writers, musicians, chemists, experimenters in colours, excellent dancers and acute observers of reality, named Frederick Scalllibur and his long life companion Hèléne Coqcuet, who boldly affirm in their *Brief History of Literature and Neurosis*, Volume 587326, page 981756, column 3874, line 8379287, that all writing is but neurosis."

---

100 It is worth remembering the writer's eagerness to invent new terms.

We then jump some pages forward, to read:

"Making a remarkably good use of this previous example, I serve myself a portion from this massive yet tasty and juicy psychological feast (the recently quoted book), in the first place because it really looks quite appetising; in second place because I'm really hungry; and in the third place, because it's a perfect and accurate description of the mental state in which the Grimm brothers were when they wrote some of their most celebrated stories.[101]

"This behavioural *pathos* most likely finds its origin at a certain point in time; precisely just five days after one of the Grimm *Gebrüder* came into this dark and sombre world,[102] when

---

101 The fourth and successive places are ignored because they do not qualify for a medal (Ed.).

102 It is not quite clear yet whether they were abandoned during the fifth day after Jacob Ludwig Karl's birth (4th of January 1785) or during the fifth day after Wilhelm Karl's birth (24th February 1786). It is worth noting that Jacob Ludwig Karl could have been abandoned during the fifth day after Wilhelm Karl's birth, or, around way other the. It well could have been after the fifth day of Ludwig van Beethoven's birth, but in order to make this possible, the abandoner, that is the *Mutter*, must have been able to travel through space and time, or perhaps Beethoven could have been born a year later. Maybe they were left abandoned during the fifth day of some unknown poor wretch's birth, whose existence we might have overlooked. Nonetheless, it is more than likely that in Beethoven's fifth symphony lie the keys to this mystery: fate banging on the door, unsparingly. Did Luigi know what was about to occur in the vicinity of his own birth? The explanations are probably infinite. So are the possibilities. But nor the ink nor the paper are neither of those things. (TN.)

their infamous *Mutter* abandoned them at the very gates of the Philippsruhe Palace of Hanau. Dorothea Zimmer was her name. It is still widely believed in their hometown of Hanau that the wicked woman intended to leave them at those very gates five days before giving birth (successfully at last) to the youngest of the two future storytellers; something she tried several times, but that lastly proved impossible. Despite the useless efforts that the abandoning mother invested in sweaty, noisy and smelly pushes, the only thing that came out of her body was a deficiently digested *Kassler Rippchen* and other UFF (Unidentified Falling Faeces).

"I do predict that in some unforeseeable future some useless translator will create an unnecessary footnote for this above-written paragraph in order to confuse and puzzle the good-faithed reader; it is easy to understand that both brothers were abandoned only once the youngest had been born. In the same fashion, contrary to all rules about good writing and logically structured literature, I simply state that the reason for the abandonment of the Grimm siblings was not a matter of grave psychological depth, but just that she was insane or OOHFM (out of her fucking mind).

"Nonetheless, it is easy to understand and to recognize why such an occurrence had been carved in their emotional memory ever since, thus provoking in the little brothers' conscious, subconscious, sub-sub-subconscious and subterranean conscious minds a huge impact. Nevertheless, they both survived the maternal abandonment: well done, little chaps!

"How was this unique feature accomplished?

"They managed to do so by mimicking pigeons,[103] those undesirable flying creatures which always manage to find some food, pecking out the scarce breadcrumbs that the old retired fellows slowly and kindly placed on the ground, in the belief that the estranged brothers were some kind of Colombian oviparous creatures that had been imported by the *Führer*.[104] We can easily see and understand how this traumatic solitary upbringing (and probably any other chapter of their lives as well) fuelled their creativity, which is reflected upon, probably at its best, in their most famous and immortal tale: *Hänsel und Gretel.* I am forced to assume that due to the lack of a strong masculine figure, a

---

103 Fact that probably inspired the late appearance of the white swan at the ending of Hänsel und Gretel's tale. Lohengrin's *Schwan* should be also included; something that speaks very highly of Richard Wagner, who suffered an indolent gesture from the Count himself yet never held the incident against the brothers Grimm.

104 It is not explicit to which *Führer* the writer is referring. Given that *Führer* means a lot of different words in English, the scope being so wide, that we could consider a bus driver, or Hitler himself. If that were indeed the case, time-travel and precognition cannot be discounted: was Count Edmund a super-human?

father-godly presence in his life, Jacob was to be immortalized as Gretel.

"Despite the horrendous abandonment they suffered, that very same happening inspired them (both being ignorant of the origin of such a vocation) to investigate, collect and write stories mainly for little children, with the laudable intention of creating impacts and nourishment for those tiny (yet) uncorrupted minds that would inevitably be exposed to adult brutality and conditioning disdain. A remarkable tale in its own right that shows how opposites can, on occasion, work towards the same useful goal.

"Once they struggled into adulthood after passing the hell of their infancy and primal teenage years, and despite being terribly busy with their frantic researches, compilations and writing (an attitude that probably reveals more about what they did not want to dwell on, rather than a positive appetite), revenge was the daily mantra that kept pecking both their conscious, subconscious and sub-sub-subconscious minds, despite the fact that neither of them had any crumbs left on their heads. It is fair to say that, deep inside, both *Gebrüder* felt that the word revenge – *Rache* in German – was not as strong and expressive enough to accurately describe the task at hand... or shall we say wing?

"In order to solve these linguistic problems, they resorted to the Italian blood present on

157

their mother's side: the *bisnonno* Giancarlo Manfredi, an exquisite *pizzaiolo* from Ascoli.

"After days of turbulent travelling, they finally found the word they were looking for, almost with a tribal fervour: *vendetta*.

"Also, by chance (if there is such a thing, and if indeed it is a thing) they finally tasted Giancarlo's doughy delicacy; the result was amazing for their taste buds yet horrendous for both their ejective orifices: their way back home was not signalled with crumbs nor shining stones, but through the thundering force and stench of the remains belonging to those barely digested pizzas.

"But despite the trials and tribulations generously offered by the digestive ordeal – which was probably caused by the ingestion of the aforementioned dough that was carrying within a single cell or perchance a couple of hairs (pubic or axillary) or some alchemical drops of Giancarlo's sweat – this acted as a catalyst for the bitter and almost liquid eruptive intestinal reaction in the *Gebrüder*: perchance itself a metaphor for something that had yet to be digested not only on a physical and obvious level but on an emotional one as well; yet, despite all those shortcomings, the aim, the daily mantra remained the same: *Rache! Vendetta!*

"A debt was finally paid during the course of a dark spring-like morning on the twenty-seventh day of the fourth month of the year 1937, in a suburb of Dresden called Aufkassental; though it is fair to affirm that the benefactor still remains in the shadows, probably because of what you are about to read. And how much would I have preferred to write *The* debt and not simply *A* debt; and surely, dear reader, you shall understand the heavy shadow that overwhelms my heart whilst I write the following explanation: within the realms of a humble abode located at 65 Haupstrasse, and locked inside a ferocious iron oven, Frau Hannelore Herzfritz died from asphyxiation, to then be slowly cooked away.

"Regrettably, the innocent woman never knew the reason why she was ultimately banished from life in her own beloved cooking device; nor did the *Gebrüder* Grimm ever truly comprehend that the demised lady was not their *Mutter*. Perhaps the storyteller brothers never found out about the occurrence, and hence never went out to celebrate the assassination; alas, one does wonder: would it be licit to imagine that even if they had indeed discovered the news about such a dreadful occurrence, they would surely not have celebrated, perhaps due to shame or guilt? Is it plausible to infer that the *Gebrüder* were no longer alive during the year 1937? What if, oblivious of the heated killing, they did mistakenly celebrate another deed that has nothing to do with what has arisen as a matter of true fictional discussion?

"Of course, given the bits and pieces of information that we are lacking, we cannot assert that they ever found out, not only about the overcooked body of the supposed-to-be-guilty mother (we ought to remind you that the wretched brother's *Mutter*'s name was Dorothea Zimmer and not Hannelore Herzfritz nor Alejandra Domínguez), but also about the horrendous mistake; yet it is nevertheless fair to guess that the shadowy benefactor wanted to share his – or her – supposed act of generosity, perhaps as an offering for his (or her) most favourite authors. The whereabouts of the abandonmental Dorothea were, are and will be an inscrutable mystery.

"At least we know that a robust and imbecile woodcutter called Manfred Grimminzschaffenthal once was the absent and ignorant[105] *Vater*; a merciful falling fir tree ended his miserable and obscure life whilst the obliviated *Gebrüder* were barely beginning to place their tiny feet on this impeccable earth, thus taking their first and solitary steps into their cruel motherless existence, begging the elderly for some miser breadcrumbs whilst mimicking the far more experienced pigeons.

---

105 It is widely assumed that poor Manfred was oblivious of their existence: i.e. he was not aware of being the father of the genius siblings.

"Then, what about the tragic ending of the bonded siblings Grimm?

"Jacob died of indigestion after enjoying (and suffering) an orgiastic engorgement of colossal amounts of chocolate brownies mixed with some good old Jamaican ganja, which was all inspired by the myth of the *Principe Azzurro*; yet, on this occasion the spell was supposed to occur through the arts and tastes of the dark delicacy alchemised with the mythical cannabis rather than the blueish Gorgonzola. Apparently, the secret intention behind this high chocolatey feast was to obtain a faster set of muscles rather than those which had been given by nature to the insecure and slow Jacob, who always lost in the brotherly races; he reasoned that if the *Principe Azzurro* was in effect blue given the insane amounts of the blue dairy delicacy, the answer to his speed insecurity would obviously be to resort to a certain food-mix that would blacken (*alla* Jamaican) him, with the firm intention of becoming – luckily – a fast and muscular and athletic dark-skinned chap.

"The Swiss milky chocolatey exquisiteness which acted as the starter had been a gift from his dear friend Heidi, who at the time used to live with her lovely grandfather, known in the village as Alm-Onji, in the Swiss Alps. According to Wilhelm's rough and grieving estimations, that very same night Jacob had tasted *circa* 9.846.365 brownie portions, each of them weighting 786 ounces. Many years later, whilst lying on her deathbed and using the last breaths available to her, Heidi contradicted the grieving and calculating *Brüder*, asserting that Jacob had only eaten 9.846.364 portions of brownie.[106]

"Tragedy had still one card to play: Wilhelm died of food poisoning after eating a cheese gone bad[107] that *der kleine* Peter, a humble goatherd who also was a dear friend of Heidi, had offered the late Wilhelm as a gift for his seventy-third birthday.

"Apparently, and according to Peter's statement, which was pronounced during the hefty hours he had to endure at the *Gestapo* headquarters, the insistent heat to which the dairy cheesy product was exposed during the crossing that the shaveling had to undertake from Mainz – his maternal home town – up to the soon-to-be-intoxicated writer's home in Berlin, could have provoked a deadly chemical

---

106 This matter kept Wilhelm and Heidi bitterly (with almonds) at odds. This distance lasted no more than three minutes; the exact number of instants that took the unavoidable Death to catch the surrendered Heidi, after she had pronounced the offensive rebuttal.

107 The English language is one that offers endless chances to create jokes based on common expressions. When we read *cheese gone bad* it's not a description of the cheese's inclination of character or reprehensible behaviour, such as: bullying smaller cheeses, or refusing to dance with a slice of *prosciutto* embraced by two halves of *baguette*; it is simply a depiction of its mouldy and contaminated deadly state.

reaction within the cheese itself. This precise theory hinted at by the naive Peter proved to be his death sentence.

"For the guardians of the law, it was clear that he knew beforehand the effect that the sun would unleash in his dairy birthday gift. As the avenging bullet was just about to leave its container, and splatter *kleine* Peter's brains on the execution wall, a phone call extended the doomed goatherd's life; at least for a few more anguished days filled with fasting and urine smell. He was illiterate but not a fool; he knew at once that his inevitable death had only been postponed; he also prefigured that only a man of immense power could stop an impending execution.

"Some days after, which for him seemed like a tiresome eternity, his famished body was baptised by the caresses of nine Nazi bullets spat by Goebbels' Luger P08 who, it is worthy of remarking, was himself a particularly truthful admirer of the extinguished *Gebrüder* Grimm.

"Joseph Goebbels had had, from the very moment his eyes first laid on a page written by the wretched brothers, a certain weakness for Jacob, perhaps inspired and fuelled by a coincidence in their flamboyant garmental predilections and unprejudiced behaviour. Maybe they shared some anatomical insecurities related to their lack of speed and, perchance, certain chocolatey passions.

"Thence, lured by Jacob's liberal choices, the *Reich Minister* used to surprise people far and wide, be that for his wardrobe choices or his ultra-*provocateur* way of walking; he would even delight the very same *Führer* during the famous Nazi's *Samstag soirées*.

"During those festive and somehow naughty Saturday *matinées*, our propagandist and executioner Paul Joseph Goebbels would dress up as a woman, preferably wearing a pink satin gown – commando style – yet covering the whole combo with the furs of some fluffy Siberian animal; and mounted on ten inch heels, dancing and shouting at the rhythm of what later shall become known as Hier an Rhein und Ruhr und in Westfalen, Dr Paul Joseph's home-region anthem.

"During these erotic meetings, he insisted on being called by his *nom de guerre*, Gretel.

"Such was the impact that this little cabaretesque number had produced in the Nazi guts, that even during the most dramatic moments of the Germanic history experienced in Hitler's bunker, there was always in its midst some kind of musical presence. Before condemning himself to an eternity of suffering, the *Führer* himself asked for his right hand and friend to arrange a little musical amusement for him. The faithful Goebbels gathered what was left of Hitler's personal choir, and intoned, whilst conducting it masterfully, the hymn *Heil, meine Gretel, meine liebere Gretel und Schokolade Gretel.*

"Still today some bootleg copies of the original phonographic registration can be bought at the *Sonntag Markt*, by the gates of the Philippsruhe Palace of Hanau.

"In an indefinite time, but in a definite place called Hamburg, Heidi was doomed to be found lifeless, buried in a half-excavated common grave, with an axe stuck in her hollowed chest and an inscription written in blood across her forehead where once the following words could be read, according to a trustworthy yet tired and cataracted man, who was overwhelmed by forgetfulness: *Grimm für immer!*

"Manfred is the supposed name of the axe executioner; an avenging woodcutter or *Vater* who actually had not really died but was only gravely wounded in that previously mentioned fir tree accident. He is thought to be still alive and inhabiting a little but well-decorated cabin, sharing his last dying days with Heidi's *Opa* in an uncharted region of the Rhein. The childless couple survive solely on a chocolate-based diet and, whenever scarcity shows its anguished face, they alternately try to commit suicide by locking themselves up inside the oven; needless to say that there is no gas, nor wood that could feed the harmless cooking device and fulfil their dying wishes.

"With the intention of bettering their situation, both are said to be planning the grand opening of a breeding ground for swans, which will be sold at retail price to children's storytellers.

"Nonetheless, I, the Count Edmund – alongside my many alter-egos – declare that the Grimm brothers were, in reality, the illegitimate sons that Heidi created with *kleine* Peter. In order to really understand the literary challenge which has been presented to your eyes, dear reader, please do try to interchange Dorothea for Rigoberto; and where a comma (,) lies, please replace it with the word delirium; do not forget to sing the entire Ring Cycle composed by Richard Wagner, yet half a tone lower, and from memory. Therein lies the answer to the riddle."

Radamés Washington "π" Funes Da Silva lightly mentions that he came across a Count Edmund von der Golz at a *trattoria* in Montevideo, but because he has nothing to do with the previous story, he calls himself to a thunderously expressive writer's silence.

Suburbial Sin

A rrogance is one of the many faces of ignorance.

It may be, perhaps, the exaggerated assessment of a simple characteristic which is believed to be one's own possession, when in reality it is simply loaned for both an unknown period of time and purpose.

Arrogance is to believe that the previous words are my own invention.

Kiss

The great and mythical Arthur, King of the Britons, sheltered by the tired shade of a tree during a strangely scorching summer afternoon, declared sententiously:

"A bad kiss is as useless to love as a wet log is to a bonfire."

Lord Edgard Murray of Melbury thus clarifies:

Such a sentence could well find its own origin in the peculiar skill, whose owner was a Dorothea of Castlecorr – a supposed 'special' friend of Arthur who, as reason dictates, could have been the very first female to enjoy the fleshy lips and lingual gifts of our epic hero – of kissing horrendously. This precise incident – bathed in that clumsiness typical of inexperience – is, in my humble opinion, that which could have inspired our callous hero to adopt a daring and decidedly pragmatic behaviour with the females, given his precious labiolingual sensitivity and great respect – almost reverential – that he showed towards the (ideally) loving act of kissing: he insisted – and therefore kissed albeit with her full consent – to the circumstantial female with whom he had established at least a close acquaintanceship or a firm friendship,[108] with the sole intention of being able to immediately dismiss all those who did not possess the secret of love on their lips and tongue. Geneva, at least for a while, was the chosen one.

If a simple grain of sand contains the entire universe, a real kiss contains the past, present and future of love; its most perfect token, its most complete symbol.

Anonymous

---

108 Needless to say, the close labiolingual relationship took place only if he found her pleasing both to his senses and to each emotional centre of his exalted being... Yet, if she had enormous tits, he would dig in without hesitation and without losing even a second in explaining his philosophical approaches and his thoughts about the divine nature of the kiss. As he famously once said: when in doubt... take it out. We assume he was referring to the tongue, and not to the...

Caravan

Onfused after finding out about the multiple existence of different schools belonging to the great spiritual tradition of humans – denominated at some point in time through the word Sufi – which were flourishing in my momentary hometown Istanbul, as well as the big Bektashi, Jerrahi, Mevlevi and Naqshbandi orders, I asked my beloved grandfather about this apparent contradiction.

His words were:

There is only one destination to which all the caravans that for centuries have been treading on the path of the great tradition are heading towards. Each one of them is composed of camels, dromedaries, or of horses or mules; some transport groceries, other treasures, other spices...yet all carry within the true nourishment of humankind.

Their guides are, only in appearance, different; so are their methods to carry forward an enterprise which has existed since the dawn of time.

The shapes, the garments, the customs and routines of each caravan are mere external accidents which say nothing of the essence... which is unique.

The multiplicity of which you talk is irrelevant to you, my beloved grandson; there is one and only one caravan whose guide has your name carved in his heart.

Seek him, for there shall be your caravan... awaiting you.

About the Author

Abu Kasem is made of sand; a man of the desert. He is also made of stars, a man from the eleven skies. He is a man that came to realise that his very essence is that of all those things that have ever lived; he knows that he is one, and he is all; he is none. He tastes the flavour of all human history in each tear and drop of sweat.

He became Abu Kasem when he discovered that the entire memory of the universe was flowing within himself, within ourselves; sharing, giving, offering infinite chances for a never-ending creation of life disguised as art. Abu Kasem is made of sand, and of stars; he lives within those very eyes that are reading these humble introductory lines, that same imagination that pictures him in his workshop, creating new words, stories, humoristic views to share: these are his alchemic essences.

Website: www.abukasem.com
Twitter: www.twitter.com/abukasem786
Instagram: www.instagram.com/abukasem786
Facebook: https://www.facebook.com/
AbukasemTheGreedyPerfumer/
YouTube Channel: https://abukasem.com/YouTube